CARTRIDGE-CASE LAW

Old Man James was cattle-baron boss – not of the town alone, but of the whole damn county; and a pretty tough hombre in his own right.

His men were Texans, every last one of them, and would no more worry about killing a guy than they would about worms in their biscuits.

The Marshal and his deputy had to take on the whole gang – even if it killed them, which it probably would . . .

OTHER NELSON NYE
TITLES IN LARGE PRINT

CARTRIDGE-CASE LAW

CARTRIDGE-CASE LAW

by
Nelson Nye

MAGNA PRINT BOOKS
Long Preston, North Yorkshire,
England.

British Library Cataloguing in Publication Data

Nye, Nelson
  Cartridge-case law.

ISBN 1-85057-736-6

Published in Large Print 1990 by arrangement with the copyright holder.

Printed and Bound in Great Britain by
Redwood Press Limited, Melksham, Wiltshire.

For
Donald Coyle
– a great hand with the organ

Chapter One

"When I Run Cattle—"

"BY the Gods" I said, "if that's all the so-an'-so's hired me for he can stick his badge up his adenoids!" and I was flinging around to stamp out of the place when Lou Gromm came through the door.

He was a tall man, Lou, with a cougar grace and teeth well matching the shine of his star. He said, "What's the matter now, Flash?" and I told him flat – both barrels.

I said: "I'm plumb fed up with your skulldraggin' chores! If you're figurin' to jail that rattle-brained fool you can go fetch him in without my help! Hear me, Lou? – I won't have no damn part of it!"

Lou Gromm – he was marshal of Galeyville – nodded. Gave me one of his bully-puss smiles. "That's quite all right," he told me; and Jose Cuervo chuckled. "You needn't to soil your lily-white hands. Nor your lily-white conscience either. Jack's curled up on a jail cot now. I've just finished locking him up."

I gave him a stare.

But Lou only widened his hair-lipped grin. 'Picked him up myself. Found him asleep in a packing crate out back of Dall's saloon."

"Must of taken real courage," I told him, "to arrest a drunk old has-been while the poor fool was snoozin' it off."

Lou ignored my tone. "When I go after a man, I get him. Any damn way that I'm able. Just remember that, Marlatt. Long as I'm marshaling Galeyville these owlhooters better step easy."

That was good for a belly laugh any day. Everyone knew Lou and Curly Bill Graham – alias Brocius, and God knew how many other fake names – was thicker than splatter or fiddlers in hell.

I screwed up my mouth and spat at a knothole. "Cherokee Jack is a goddam fool – even *you*'ll admit that. But he ain't no cut-an'-run killer. Even a kid in three-cornered pants would have more savvy than to gut-shoot a—"

"You can't out-talk the evidence, Flash."

"*What* evidence?"

"You'll find out when they hold the inquest," Lou smiled. "I've got Jack

10

hogtied proper."

"Got him framed, you mean," I said with a sneer; but Lou kept a hold of his temper.

"I don't have to frame him. He did it."

Weak Back murmured tired-like, "Goin' to take Hack Averill's word for it, are you?" and Lou came right back hard at him.

"I don't have to take nobody's word for anything. I run this town like it suits me," he said.

And, with another cold smile, walked out.

In the marshal's office there wasn't no sound for eight or ten seconds hand-running. Then Weak Back shifted his lard-bucket haunches and scowled roundabout him disgusted. "It's a-comin'," he said. "Yes, sir, it sure is a-comin'. One of these days we're a-goin' to find Lou croaked with a knife in his back."

Blowing out his cheeks he looked across at me. "You didn't know Lou in the ol' days, did you?"

"Not before Lincoln, if that's what you mean."

"No," he said, "I'm speakin' o' San Saba. Why – only so far back as Charleston they'll tell you how Lou was a heller. The real, red striped variety. With the women, I mean.

Always after 'em – couldn't never let 'em alone. Hitched fast or single, it was all one to Lou; an' he ain't changed none for the better. Ever hear the cold deck he run in on Dirk Harrigan? You ought've. Quite a passel of talk at the time, I remember . . . Him an' ol' Dirk they was pardners, them days, runnin' cattle wet fr'm Sonora. Lou taken a shine t' Dirk's woman, they claim, an' one night when Dirk was across the river Lou grabbed her up an' run off with 'er. But he left a note for the Law to work on. It got Dirk nabbed by the Border Patrol – caught him flat with a whole herd of critters . . . Guess he's still doin' time for it."

I wasn't much interested in Lou's past didos. It was what he was up to now that puzzled me. I scowled. "About old Cherokee," I said – "do you reckon Lou'll sure-enough rail him?"

"Why not? Lou's wantin' reappointment, ain't he? What's Jack t' him? Nothin' t' lose no sleep over – an' a real advantage once he's got Jack dead. What Lou wants," Weak Back told us, "is a goat fer Cramp Leyholt's killin'."

"But hell," I said; "ol' Cherokee ain't got enough wits t' kill a fly!"

"All the better fer Lou then." Weak Back

12

leaned forward to tap my knee. "You mark my word. Jack's as good as buried."

"Mebbe," I said; "but there might come a slip betwixt this jail an' the rope . . ."

I grunted, got up and let the rest trail off. The way a fellow will, sometimes, I looked over at the clock. And met Cuervo's stare. Jose Cuervo was the third of us deputies, and oldest by point of hiring. An odd, little dapper squirt of a guy that, mostly, got along good with us – good, any way, as you could expect of a greaser. But he wasn't very bright in the head, we figured, and some of his stares was enough to freeze you.

He had a real vacant look to his eyeballs now.

"I guess I'll go feed my tapeworm," I said.

There was knots of idling men on the street – there was only one street in Galeyville; over there front of Jack Dall's place, and by the hitchrack fronting McConaghey's. Fellows with their hats lapping over each other's, talking real soft-like – muttering. Cooking up some new kind of deviltry, likely. For this Galeyville was a boom silver camp, Curly Bill's new stronghold; and God only knew what its end

13

would be. Jim Hughes told me once it was the healthiest camp in the Territory. Which it maybe was. But it kept three sawbones sweating continual keeping its hardcase boosters patched up, and there was talk already of moving Boot Hill though the camp was not yet four months old.

The sun smashed down with summer's fury. Nothing seemed to have changed any great amount since morning. The creek still gurgled round the mesa's foot and black smoke boiled from the smelter with a perfume akin to fresh brimstone. The long main street (there *was* a few trails leading off of it) run square with the creek, but above it, along the mesa's rim with its stores, saloons and honkey-tonks all crowding the far side doggedly, like they was scared a splash of water might hurt them. All but one, that is – the biggest of them all; the dive run by Nick Babcock. Curly Bill's hangout. A place notorious for the poorness of its booze, its roughhouse brawls and loose women.

As my glance played over the street this noon I kind of wondered which of these argufying hombres standing round might be the old friend Tilt James was expecting, the fellow he said was coming up from Saba.

14

Then I chanced to look across towards Nick Babcock's.

Curley Bill Graham was sitting out front, taking his ease in Nick's rocker. He had one paw around a bottle of beer. A six-shooter banged in the other every time he saw a trade rat, or a gopher strayed out of its burrow.

He was a damn tough monkey and a friend of Lou Gromm's, but I sung my voice out anyhow. "Cut it out," I yelled, "before you hit somebody!" and the old rip drove a slug past my shoulder.

For two cents I'd of gone over and clouted him one; and I thought some of doing it anyhow till I caught the glint of his eyeballs. Then I decided to ignore him – kind of turn the other cheek. He looked primed enough to kill somebody, and I knew by experience if that thought and him ever come to meet up there was nothing this side of hell could stop him. Besides, I'd just finished planting Cramp Leyholt. Which was digging enough for one morning.

I left him spinning his gun by the guard and got me a stool in Jukk's hash house. It was pretty fair crowded, with the whole crew talking, and I kept my ears skinned as a matter of principle. I was *one* fool lawman

15

what aimed to earn his money. It wouldn't be the first time I'd picked up news that had stood Lou Gromm in good stead.

Don't get the idea I was snooping. I was just making myself receptive.

I digested the talk along with my meal; and then I went back to the office.

Weak Back was just coming out. He stopped, mopped his face with an unbuttoned shirtsleeve. Then he spat out his chaw. He said disgusted-like, "Can't figure out how you do it, Flash – they sure don't wait on *me* none!"

I shoved a puzzled look round after him. Then I sighted the rig that was tied front of Shotwell's. One look was aplenty. I hurried on in.

She was there, all right. Careless leaned against Lou's desk. She was fanning the heat with a reward bill.

"Flash!"

"Yours truly," I said, and chuckled.

She was the best looking goods in the Cherrycows. My eyes must've told her I thought so, I reckon, for she flushed up like she most always did every time we got together this way. But she didn't say "Darling!" like it was her custom when there wasn't no one else round us. Nor she didn't

16

come forward to catch my hand, nor anything else like usual.

She stood where she was, leaned against Lou's desk, with the sun's glint bright in her hair. The skin of her cheeks was gone tight and pink. There was an odd kind of look in her stare.

"What's the matter," I said, "is there somethin' gone wrong? Lost your pet mocker, or such like?"

She said, "Flash – what's Gromm doing about those miners?"

So that was it. Them miners again.

I heaved me a sigh and fished out the makings. If there was any one thing her old man couldn't abide it was what he called 'gopher-hole' miners.

Tiltpot James was a brass-collar dog in these here mountain environments; the biggest rancher in this whole stretch of country, and about as cantankerous as a pulque-drunk squaw. He owned the Cherrycow Cattle Company. This town, truth to tell, was squatted plumb on his range – right in the midst of the best of it. Which was a heap bad enough in its own right, but not the worst by a jugful. The prospecting breed was scattered all through these rimrocks, gophering his graze and scaring off stock till the old man was fit to be hog-tied. Had his ax all dug up and sharpened and was glaring around like a ory-eyed bull just waiting for someone to cross him. Point was, he blamed the marshal's office. Which was kind of narrow-minded, it seemed like to me, even if Lou *had* got them diggers in here. He had, right enough – and Tilt knew it. I could tell, all right, hell would soon enough pop; old Tilt James was a he-kanga-roo which would have his way and be damned to you. Meaner than gar soup thickened with tadpoles. Unreasonable – there wasn't no word for it.

"Uh . . . You better talk to Lou," I said, soothing. "He'll be back from—"

"I'm talking to *you*, Flash Marlatt! And don't you give me no ring-around. I'm expecting a decent answer!"

"Well . . . good gosh!" I said, and licked my smoke the whiles I was hunting a match up and scratching like blazes for something to say which wouldn't touch off no fireworks.

I don't want you to get me wrong now. Dora James was a mighty fine girl – the finest dang girl in the Cherrycows. But she was a Texan, too, and the toast of the range, with an old man bigger than Billy-be-damn.

18

Which, mebbe, had give her some notions. Like a kid with a new red wagon.

So I tried my hand at diplomacy. I said, "Dora – have you et?" and knew right off I was in for it.

But I wasn't – not then.

Boot sound scuffed the planks outside and Lou Gromm, flashing an oily smile, come in like we was making a compliment on him.

Dora snatched up her parasol. There ain't no word for the look she give him. But before she could unlimber any choice remarks old Tilt, himself, come traipsing in, with Weak Back lumbering after him.

Tilt wasn't wasting no time. He lashed right out like a Kansas twister.

"What's this I hear about you an' them hole diggers? What the blankety-blank blank—"

"If you've heard it," Lou drawled, "why come bawling to me?"

You could see the sparks blazing old Tilt's stare, and his voice croaked like a frog had got in it. "Don't peddle that stuff to *me*, Lou Gromm! The cow vote put you in office – an' by God it can yank you out again, too! You'll take your orders from me an' like 'em or I'll damn well run you out of the country!"

19

The old man had a burly shape and could twist bar iron like baling wire. A tangle of uncombed, brick-colored hair spilled across his forehead from under his hat, and the gun barrel stare aglint beneath it made a Paiute on the warpath look plumb gentle as a tumblebug. His face was so red I thought he would choke.

But he didn't. He said, like his talk was all scrinched up: "I've heard you been locatin' prospectors—"

"If you know so much about it," Lou sneered; but old Tilt never let him finish. With a roar he said:

"By God! You *admit* it?"

"Sure."

Lou laughed like a Injun. Lips peeled back and no more sound than a spider. I expect he was part Injun; I've heard tell his Maw's folks wore moccasins.

He dropped his humor, of a sudden, and scowled.

"Sure I been locatin' 'em. I'll locate every footloose Jack that's got any money to pay me for it. You don't like it, eh?"

I looked for Tilt to bust his buttons. His cheeks got the color of horseturd red. He gasped. He gurgled. His scarred fists clenched till I thought they'd pop; and I held my breath for his bellow.

But he said, real soft and quiet-like, "When I run cattle it's to make money, mostly. I can't make money with these silver-plated shop clerks chousin' my cows off and pockin' my range up with prospect holes. So looky, Lou – you tell these little playmates of yours to take their diggers an' git someplace else. You tell 'em to git in a hurry, too, because soon's I'm back I'm havin' the Cherrycows shoot every pick-swinger sighted."

Chapter Two

Blood On The Moon

I HELD my breath and squinched myself as far out of line as possible.

But the fireworks didn't come.

Which was strange, when you come to think of it, because both them fellers was pretty big guns, and they'd both of them meant what they'd shouted. Lou and Curly Bill had come here together right after John Galey had opened it up; and Lou had been

21

rodding it ever since – with Curly Bill's help and approval, of course, for Bill had made this place his headquarters since he'd got in wrong with the Earps and quit Tombstone. Curly Bill's whole bunch was at Lou's beck and call, and he didn't give a damn who knew it.

But old man James was cattle baron boss – not of the town, but the whole damn country; and a pretty tough egg in his own right. He owned the biggest spread in the Territory and his men was no kind to yell 'Boo!' at. They was Texans – every last one of them, and would no more worry about killing a guy than they would about worms in their biscuits.

Just the same, there wasn't no fireworks.

"Go ahead," Lou sneered in his hair-lip-ped way, "an' we'll see which end of the stick you've got. This town's fed up with your mighty ways. Don't start nothing you can't finish—"

"Can't finish!" That was when the old man let go. You could of heard him clean to the Sulphur Springs Valley. "Can't finish!" he howled. "Why, bless you, Gromm, I'll finish this whole damn town for you! I'll wind this place up so quick and so slick folks'll think it was only a legend! *Can't finish!*" he roared. "Why, you belly-crawlin' sidewinder – I'll smash your town plumb into the dust an' make you into hog meat!"

I looked at Weak Back and Weak Back shrugged. I sighed and went tramping out after them. They was heading slam-bang for their wagon that was tied out front of Ike Shotwell's store. I picked a paper scrap up off the doorstep, the way an observing man will sometimes; absently stuffed the thing into my pocket.

I trailed them over to Shotwell's then, to where their team was tied to Ike's hitch rack.

Tilt looked mad enough to chaw the sights off a sixgun. He never even noticed me tagging alongside. He was muttering into his whiskers, and I let him keep right at it while I said soothing things to Dora.

She wasn't a heap receptive.

But I knew how sweet she could really be when she wasn't fretted up about her father. Probably just a mite peeved with me, I figured, account of it likely seemed I had stuck up for Lou – which I hadn't, of course. Not really. But I would of, though, if he'd give me an invite. Far as them miners come into it, anyhow. They had as much rights on this range as old James had. He *controlled* the country but he didn't own it. I had chased cows' tails off and on, myself; but I didn't think cows was everything.

I took a quick look at Dora, slanchways.

She sure looked cute with her taffy hair, her bright, sparkly eyes and beaded buckskins. 'Course, a parasol didn't rightly go with buckskins. But that was the James in her – the Tiltpot part. A James could get away with things no other man would dast dream of.

Only one way to handle a James, I figured. When they was mad, make out like they wasn't. "Dora," I said, like all was forgiven, "I'll be out tomorr—"

And that was when Tilt noticed me. He was halfway into the wagon seat. He turned clear round and got back down with a face that was black as thunder.

"You won't if you value your health," he said. "Keep plumb away from my place – you hear? No slat-sided snake from Lou Gromm's office is goin' t' marry into *my* fambly! Not by the Seven Hinges! Try comin' around an' you'll go back feet first. On a shutter, by grab! Is that plain enough?"

I might of argued, of course. But with Tilt James' jaw half an inch from your own, with his flippers clenched and his daughter watching, only a fool would make out to be obstinate. Be a heap too much like kicking Giant Powder. If I'd known what was coming . . . Well, if folks could look ahead a ways there'd be a heap of things done different, I reckon. Probably just as well that we can't, like enough; we might spend all our time hunting holes to crawl into.

Anyhow, I didn't give him no lip.

I heaved me up a real doleful sigh, said good-bye to Dora with a daunsy look and got away from his wagon.

I ambled round aimless, then struck back for the office, it having come to my mind it was time we was letting Ed Roach out. Roach was a new one to Galeyville. He had started out with a real talent. A drifter, he was, that Weak Back had put in the cooler for smashing McConaghey's bar mirror. He was the only gent we'd had in the jug till Lou had shoved Cherokee Jack in.

The office was crowded with miners. You never heard such a hubbub as those fellows made. The place was packed like a sardine can and their noise was like hell on cart

25

wheels.

Lou was there and his eyes was black.

"Shut up!" he snarled at them finally. "We'll talk this over *calmly,* or we won't talk it over at all! . . . Now, John," he said as the roar died away, "you look like you still got hold of your wits. See if you can tell me what it's all about."

John Galey, he was speaking to.

I knew old John pretty well them days. Square a man as you'd hope to find – it was him the town had been named for. He'd come out from Pennsylvania and was owner of the discovery mine. It was him had put up the smelter.

"Well, I'll tell you," old John said, thinking it over. "We been threatened. I guess you'd call it a threat, anyways. Tilt James come down and – But here! Hold on – I've got the thing here in my pocket."

He took out a paper. Pushed it over to Lou. "There you are. That's what started the commotion. Tilt tacked it on the smelter-house door."

Lou gave him a look, then stared at the paper. He spread it out on his desk, cheeks thinning. The cords of his neck stood out as he read and you could see his block of a chin start to jut. Then his eyes snapped up, looked around at the crowd.

When they come to me I said, "By the way, Lou—"

I'd been going to say wasn't it time we was turning that drifter loose; but Lou, looking ugly, bent again to Tilt's paper. And, seeing the way his black eyes snapped, I decided to let Mr. Roach wait a spell.

Like he thought maybe Lou couldn't read very good, one of them red-shirted miners shouts: "It says *'Close up or git busted up!'* and it's signed *The Regulators*—"

"Did the old man," Lou asked, looking at Galey, "nail this thing up personal? I mean, did any of you see him?"

"Ike Shotwell saw him."

"Ike did? When was that?"

"A short time after the noon—"

"Don't you figure," the big-mouthed miner butted in, "them Regulators—"

"I'll *regulate* them!" Lou said mighty clear like. "You boys go along back to work now. And keep your rifles handy. You've got my permission—"

"Hold on!" said old John. "We don't want any violence."

But Lou waved them all outside. "*I'll* take care of the violence," he said; and the look of his eyes was plumb wicked. You could just about see him telling himself how he aimed to take care of Mr. Tiltpot, too.

Deputy Cuervo stepped in from the jail about the time the last of them was tramping their boots out.

Lou slammed the door to shut out their yammer and Cuervo, touching his shoulder, remarked:

"Thees Cherokee Jack, she's say eef evair she's get loose of thees jail she's goin' for keel you sure."

"*Him!*" Lou snorted. "That o' fool couldn't kill a—"

He chopped the rest off quicker than scat and, with his mouth tight shut, went out.

.

"Come near tippin' the applecart *that* time," Weak Back observed, getting out his old Bowie and whittling a point on his pencil. When he got the thing sharp enough to suit him he slipped the knife back into his boot and dug out a dog-eared notebook. He kind of grunted then and cleared his throat. He said, cocking a slanchways eye at me, "I got this thing shapin' up pretty good – them first three stanzas is real ripsnorters. Be a real advantage t' hear 'em."

"Okey," I sighed. I knew there wasn't no use trying to stop him. Weak Back could be

28

right determined, some ways – special when it come to his scribblings. He was bound he was going to be a poet some day. I told him he hadn't the shape for it, but all that done was get his old Adam up. He was going to back them Eastern dudes plumb off the map; I guessed he would if he read them that stuff. Judge Burnett – him that used to be the court at Charleston – had some kind of book about tent-making. It was by a Cheyenne Injun, or something. He loaned it to Weak Back to read one time. Since then Weak Back had been going round with a vacant look and a positive mania for scribbling off jingles.

"Looks like," he said plaintive like, "you could make out to be a little mite interested. Them Eastern nabobs pays big money fer this stuff. The Judge tol' me once when he was in New Haven he went to a place that was packed to the doors with folks that had come t' hear some feller read poetry. Some of it, the Judge says, they even put to music!"

"I expect so. Where'd he say this New Haven place was?"

Weak Back eyed me like a bull eyes a flag wave. "Don't try t' git me off the subjeck. If you ain't got enough culcher to enjoy

29

good poetry, the least you kin do is let on like you have. This poem," he scowled, "is called the Ballard of Jawbone the Loose-Mouth, an' it's damn good, too, if I do say it myself. Listen—

"The' onct was a feller called Jawbone the Loose-mouth,
    A tough-hombre jasper which could draw like a flash —
He rode his cow pony right into saloons an'
    The guy tried to stop him sure hadn t' be brash.

"Ol' Jawbone, the Loose-Mouth, was thin-like an' slatted,
    His ribs was so sharp they was plain as plowed ground—
Face matted with whiskers, his boots shone like mirrors;
    His pleasure the ladies it was to astound.

"Sorta like ol' Lou, y' see."
"Yeah," I said. "Is that all?"
"Fer two cents," Weak Back muttered, "I'd wash my hands of your edgucation. 'F I didn't have no more ear f' verse'n what *you*

got – Hell!" he said. "Here's the rest of it – what I got done, I mean:

"He forked a wild mustang, a flea-bitten broncho,
A bundle of sin that was wrapped in sho't hair—
Nose curved like a compass, his teeth was like shovels;
His neigh was a blast like the snort of a bear."

"Whose?" I said. "Jawbone's?"
"No, the – You go t' hell!" snarled Weak Back huffily, and slammed himself down in Lou's chair.

It was 6 p.m. and still plenty hot when I reported back for the night shift. According to Lou's schedule I was supposed to hold down the office that night while Weak Back made the rounds of the town – not that Lou was set against hell-raising, but just to make sure that if and when the hotter regions got moved the right gents was holding the hefting bar. Meaning Curly Bill and his cronies of course.

Cuervo, going off duty, flipped me his bunch of keys and a grin. Then he jingled his spur chains off down the street, headed, I supposed, for a hash house.

I went into the office and hung up my hat.

Lou Gromm looked up and scowled sour-like. "You can put that lid back on your cabeza. I'm staying. You can have the night off—"

"Thought I heard you say you was goin' over to Tombstone?"

"Well, I ain't. So clear out. I've got some letters to write."

"Okey," I said. You could see he was in one of his sod-pawing moods, so I buttoned my lip and went down to Doaks' stable; I was sort of halfway decided to go out and see Dora.

Doaks loaned me a horse for the price of its keep and I loped off down the Turkey Creek bottoms. It was cool down there in the sycamore timber and I thought, first off, a ride would do me good. But pretty soon I got to thinking about Cherokee Jack Rogers that Lou had slapped in jail for Cramp's killing – of the deal Lou had got in store for him.

Not that the old drunk was anything to me. It was no skin off *my* nose what happened to him. Just the same, I thought, it was a sorry damn piece of business, railroading a poor old whisky-sick fool that hadn't even sense enough to sabe what was happening.

Kind of put a damper on my idea of riding.

Then I recollected what Dora's old man had said would happen next time I come pasearing out there. No sense, I thought, getting proud with James. He was a pretty good coot, when you come right down to it; let him have a couple days to cool off in and he'd likely be just as neighborly as ever. He was riled up now on account of Lou Gromm, and the prospectors Lou was getting rich steering out there. But give old Tilt a mite of time, I figured, and he'd savy plain enough I hadn't no part in it.

I was naturally put out because I wanted to see Dora, and when a fellow craves to see his girl he craves to see her without let or hindrance. But this was a time to use my head, I reckoned. Tilt was mad and, by his lights, he had plenty reason. He'd been the first white gent to settle in this valley and had had to wrest his ground from the Injuns. He couldn't see no use letting it be plumb ruined just to fatten the pockets of Galeyville's marshal. Tilt had been here

33

even before John Galey. I know, because I'd punched Tilt's cattle before Galey was heard of.

There was considerable to be said for Tiltpot James.

There wasn't nothing you could say for Galeyville. In fact, the less said the better. It was a plain, wide open, unvarnished hellhole, and wouldn't never be no better long as Curly Bill run it.

There wasn't no reasoning with Curly Bill Graham. He was one of your roughest sort; good natured long as things went his way, but all the time strictly business. That business being the forcible acquirement of things other men had worked mighty hard for.

There wasn't no mercy nor no honor in him. His heart was the colour of his hair and eyes, and he'd kill a guy just to see the squirt wiggle. He was just like frostbit dynamite.

Like most of your hardcase hellions, Curley Bill had come from Texas – away back, and for reasons not publicly quoted. Not that anybody give a damn. Arizona, in them days, was mostly being settled by fellows run out of more comfortable places. Folks didn't come here for pleasure – nor, not very often, of their own intentions. They just sort of arrived; and a man's private past wasn't much peered into. Special that of Curly Bill, who was a double-acting engine there wasn't nobody craving to tamper with.

He'd of pulled down a medal for looks anyplace. Dark complected, black eyed and black haired, with a round, swarthy face that dimpled when he laughed and showed teeth white as a nigger's. And big, he was – God-awful big. Powerful as a mule's hind legs. Great hairy chest and burly shoulders, and arms that was thick as fenceposts. He could appear almighty good natured, so long as he was having his way. But lo and behold if he wasn't! He could take on a sheen like polished jet and his way with a gun was plumb wicked.

Arizona's history and bible tracts ain't got many words in common. When they first got to talking about setting it up, the idea, they tell me, was to use red ink; but, as old John Clum pointed out to the talkers, "The's *some* words, gents, looks more fittin' in black." And the words repeated most often, you'll find is *Curly Bill* and *Brocius* – which was what the old rip claimed his name was the only time they ever got him in court.

It was right after he first showed up in this country. The court was at Tombstone and the judge's name was Gray. Curly Bill was being tried for the murder of Fred White, a marshal he'd killed. Wyatt Earp was his friend then, and Curly was cleared. Maybe Earp was too awed by what he had seen to tell the plain truth; or, maybe, he never even saw it. But the event's worth recording, for it served to introduce Curly's road-agent spin, a trick he pulled slicker than slobbers. To quote Bill's own brag – made quite some time later – he had 'salivated White deliberate'.

It was a pretty dark night when it happened. But there was plenty of light on Allen Street when Curly, with a bunch of drunk cowboy companions, stepped out from a grog shop's batwings. In a fine mood for horseplay the bunch pulled their guns and commenced driving holes through the glassware. All but Curly Bill, Bill says, who was against wasting lead on principle.

When Fred White come running to see what was up, the only gent waiting was Curly Bill Graham-Brocius. "Gimme that gun!" White demanded.

"I never done that shootin'," snarled Curly.

"Never mind. Just hand me that hogleg."

Curly Bill gave him a cold, dark look and shifted the set of his shoulders. Wyatt Earp, just then, came panting up; and Curly Bill took out his pistol. According to Earp, Earp jumped him; but Bill says that come later. Bill says he extended his pistol, butt forward, with his first finger hooked in the trigger guard. White, mollified, lowered his pistol. That was when Curly Bill flipped the gun, end for end, and fired, just as Marshal White seized it.

Which shows you the kind of a guy Bill was. Ornery as tadpoles dunked in fresh cow turd.

I could tell you a heap about Curly Bill any time – how he rode at the head of forty ripsnorters who were ripe for anything from gutting to slutting. How every crook at this end of the Territory owed some kind of allegiance to him. How he slaughtered Mex smugglers and stole their silver – how he killed Mex ranchers and stole their women – how he stole more cattle and robbed more stages than any damn crook his age in the country. I could tell you a hell's own smear of things if it wasn't I've got so many other things to tell you. But don't let them tell you Ringo was the brains. Side of Curly you could put Ringo's brains in a thimble.

But it was more of Cherokee Jack I was thinking than of Curly Bill as I rode back to Doaks' stable. He was just an old pasty-faced worm of a man; no damn good to anyone. Been a owlhoot rider with one of the gangs till he got to hitting the booze so bad he couldn't hang hold of his saddle. But, someway, I felt sorry for him. He hadn't one friend in Galeyville; he was on the outs with Curly Bill, even, having stole a mule from a woman Bill was sparking. He come near being a goner that time! "You two-bit chicken thief," Curley Bill roared. "You stole that critter off a widder in Pinery, an' you take it straight back to her an' take it back pronto. G'on! Burn the wind 'fore I make a sieve o' you!"

It was a mighty low thing, it seemed to me, the way Lou was fixing to frame him. Jack couldn't no more of killed Cramp Leyholt than he could of scratched his ear with his elbow.

I don't quite know why I tied Doaks' horse out back of the marshal's office. A man does a heap of crazy things he can't never find no reason for. Except I kind of had a idea I could maybe talk Lou out of it.

But Lou wasn't in the office.

38

There wasn't nobody in it and, sudden like, it come to me what a damn good joke it would be on Lou is somebody happened to let Jack loose.

Cuervo's keys was still snug in my pocket.

I went into the pail cell corridor.

Lantern light showed the drifter, Roach, stretched out on his cot with his belly turned wallward. His snores was enough to give a guy goosebumps.

I threw a quick look at the clock on Lou's desk.

9:45.

So be it.

It was 2:15 the next morning, and black as a stack of stovelids, when a rough hand shook me from slumber.

All I could see was a dark, bent shape; but I wasn't in no doubt who the shape belonged to. It was Jose Cuervo. There seemed something wrong with his breath, I thought; and then remembered, and enjoyed a private grin with myself.

I sat up and threw my blanket back.

Never do to let him figure I was wise to nothing.

"What's up?" I said as I reached for my

boots.

I reached for my boots but I didn't pick them up.

I didn't pick up anything because, with his teeth all a-chatter, Jose Cuervo gasped:

"The marshal, Flash! *Valgame dios!* She ees dead on the desk weeth a knife een hees back!"

Chapter Three

Hold On There, Joe

I ALLOW we ought've expected it. Weak Back had warned us it was in the cards. But, someway or another, a man never reckons the folks he knows – them people he does his eating and cussing with – is going to be took off violent.

The inquest, set for ten the next morning, was held in Babcock's bar. It was the biggest place in town – and packed. By 9:51 it was so golrammed crammed even the flies like to of lost their breath and Butterball Benton, the Coroner, come within a ace of not getting in.

He was a large and corpulent gentleman with a deal of leaf lard bulging his clothes and three chins rolling their sweat down his collar. He was usually quite willing to leave dignity for comfort and, to that end, had come in his shirt sleeves. It was a Sheba of a shirt, somewhat wilted, but clean. Thick lavender stripes pranced up and down on it – it being Butterball's notion these made him look slimmer – and against this background his undone yellow tie dangled loose and limp as the ends of a dish rag. It took the full efforts of the whole marshal's office to work his perspiring bulk through the crowd and when we got done he was heaving like a jelly. "Give 'im a drink," I said to Nick, "or we'll be all night getting started."

After downing a tumbler of Nick's tornado juice Butterball got perked up a mite. He hauled up his tie, pulled it around as was proper, and stuffed his shirt in his pants again. Then he picked up Nick's bung-starter and rapped on the polished black top of Nick's bar.

"Ladies an' *gen*'lemen!" he wheezed like a traveling medicine man. "We're gathered here . . . We are gathered here – Hell's fire! y'all know what we're here for, damn it! T' find which skunk – I mean, t' find out what killed Marshal Lou Gromm las' night. An' by godfries, we're goin' t' do it, too!"

He glared around like he was expecting some argument. Then, as nobody said nothing – except Jim Hughes who was drunk as a gopher, he remarked, "Any you gents got a feelin' f' jury duty can just step right up here alongside the bar."

Nobody said nothing. Nobody moved.

Butterball scowled. He shifted his bulk like a gnat had bit him; mopped his three chins and let his pop eyes rove the watching faces. "What the hell," he growled. "I gotta have a jury! Hey – you over there! Yeah, you. Jim Corby! Git up here – you, too, Farness. An' you, off yonder, with the horsehide vest! You, too, John; an' . . ."

He finally got enough. And after he'd got them all lined up, and had mopped his triple chins again, then, peering round, he yowled out: "John! John Galey! Git up here on this soapbox, John. We gotta ask you some questions."

Old John stared round kind of dubious. "Don't believe," he said, "I can make it, Joe."

"Nev' mind," come back Butterball, generous-like. "You can talk where y' are good as anyplace, I reckon. I want you to
42

speak right out now an' tell these boys what y' heard when y' started back into Lou's office yestiday – I mean, after you'd all cleared out an' he'd shut the door. Talk up loud now, John. These boys wants t' hear this."

" 'Fraid I don't quite catch your—"

"I want you t' say what you heard Joe Cuervo tellin' the Marshal."

"That don't hardly seem in the nature of—"

"I'll judge of that," Benton snapped. "You just tell what you heard – what you heard Cuervo tell Lou Gromm."

So old John up and told them how Cuervo, coming out of the jail room, had warned Lou about what Jack had said; how Cherokee Jack had sworn to kill Lou if he ever got out of Lou's lock-up.

Butterball said, "Now we'll hear from Mister Flash Marlatt. How about it, Flash?" he said with a wink. "You heard Cuervo, didn't you?"

I didn't like it. None whatever. I didn't like the way this was going, nor the things I seen in Butterball's eyes. But I couldn't see nothing else for it. I told them I had heard him. "However," I said, "that don't by any means *prove* nothin'. I never heard Cherokee

43

Jack say—"

"Just tell us this," cut in Butterball, banging Nick's bar with the bung-starter again. "When you was on duty at the jail las' night—"

"I wasn't on duty last night—"

"What's that?" Butterball glared round at Cuervo. "Didn't you tell me, Joe—"

"I was *supposed* to of been on duty last night, but—"

"Didn't somebody tell me," Butterball growled, "that Lou had a date – er, um . . . I mean that Lou had business over to—"

"Lou," I said, "let on like he had to go over to Tombstone last night. But he told me when I come into the office that he wasn't going an' I could have the night off. If it was a date he had, she must've changed her mind. Mebbe," I hinted, "her husban' come home."

"So you're claimin' you wasn't on duty last night?"

"I ain't claimin' nothin'," I told him short. "You asked me a question an' I answered it."

"Suppose, then," Butterball purred at me nasty, "you tell these gents where you *was* last night."

"I went for a ride—"

44

"Oh! You went for a ride, did you? Where?"

"I can't see what the hell difference that makes. *I* didn't kill Lou, if that's what you're gettin' at."

Benton just eyed me. "Seems kinda funny you can't remember—"

"If you got to know," I said, holding my temper, "I rode around through the hills."

"Oh. Did you ride through the hills all night, Mister Marlatt?"

I looked at Butterball careful. I took a good long look at him. And come to the conclusion there was a whole heap of things about the Galeyville coroner I hadn't never taken proper notice of before. I hadn't, for instance, ever thought him ambitious. It began to look now like he was a heap ambitious.

The more I eyed him, the more I wondered. Began to look like I hadn't really ever *seen* Joe Benton. Trouble was, I decided, I hadn't ever give him much thought before. Kind of taken him for granted along with the rest of the Galeyville scenery.

Which had been a mistake.

I could see that now.

"Come, come!" he growled, banging the

45

bung-starter. "Did you spend the whole night ridin' through the hills?"

"No," I said careful.

"Was you ridin' alone?"

"Yes."

"What was the matter? Couldn't you sleep?"

"I could sleep all right," I said.

"Mebbe you had some special reason to go larruping off through the hills—"

"Now look," I said, "you better get this straight. I wasn't riding over two-three hours. I was back in town by ten o'clock."

"What did you do with Doaks' horse?"

"Doaks' horse?" I said blank-like.

"Sure. The one you rented from him to take your ride."

"Why . . ." I remembered, then, I'd left him back of the marshal's office . . . I remembered a number of other things, too. I remembered, for instance, I had once regarded Butterball as a 'fat old slob' and had made no bones about saying so. I remembered I had once bid him out of a sorrel filly he had seemed to set a considerable store by. I remembered . . .

"Never mind thinking up no lies," Butterball said. "It'll be plain enough to these jurymen pretty soon what you did

46

with him." He smiled at me nasty. "What did you do after you got back to town?"

I eyed that question from a number of angles. Then I told him the truth. I said, "I dropped in on Lou. We chewed the rag—"

"He was still in a rag chewin' mood at ten, was he?"

"I said I chewed the rag with him, didn't I?"

"All right. What'd you talk about?"

I was getting pretty fed up with this. "What do most guys talk about when they're settin' round passin' the time of day? Whatever come into our minds, I reckon. Horses an' cattle. Range conditions. Things like that."

"Odd you didn't talk about minin'. Or the epidemic we got of stage-robbin' round here."

"Mebbe we did. Mebbe," I said sarcastic, "if I'd had any idee how interested you'd be I'd of kep' a diary of our conversation."

"Pity you didn't. What'd you do after that?"

"After a while," I said, "Lou got out some letters an' I read for a spell—"

"Read Lou's letters?"

"No. The *Tombstone Epitaph* – you'll find it around there somewheres if you look.

47

Unless it's sprouted wings since last night—"

"Been a mort of things sproutin' wings round here lately," said Butterball drily. "You recognize this knife?"

"I ought to. I bought it off Ike Shotwell las' fall."

"I was wonderin' if you'd admit it." Butterball craned his neck, looking round. Then "Doc—" he called, "mind tellin' this jury where you found that knife?"

Doc Cranston fingered his watch chain, thoughtful. "I found it," he said, "in the marshal's back. The blade—"

"You can tell 'em about the blade later. Right now I think we'll hear from Jose. Hey! Cuervo!" he shouted, glaring round the packed bar room. "Now where's that damfool Mex gone off to? . . . Oh, well, we'll get back to him later. Doc— Some of you gents git a path opened up there. That's it. Doc, you come up here where we can all get a look at you . . . Thanks. Now, I want you to tell these boys about las' night. About – well, start with Marlatt comin' to your house for you."

Doc Cranston dabbed at his face with his handkerchief. He was a bent little man in rusty black store clothes. He carried a brush-clawed bag in his hand. He wore steel-rimmed spectacles that was wore pretty thin from all the cleanings he give them. He gave them one now.

Then he cleared his throat.

"Mister Marlatt," he said, "knocked on the door of my house at about two-thirty. He told me Lou Gromm had been stabbed. Said Lou was at the office and would I come right over. I asked was Lou dead. He said it looked like Lou was, but I should come over anyhow. So I—"

"Git a move on, Doc," Curly Bill growled impatient. "Some of us boys has other business to tend to – some of us fellas has got t' meet that stage."

Doc Cranston eyed the burly outlaw and scowled. Then he shifted his glance and cleared his throat nervous-like. He took out his watch — jammed it back in his pocket with a look of annoyance.

Butterball asked: "What time was Lou killed?"

"I would say, from the evidence, rather close to midnight." He pursed his lips. "It would not be possible—"

"Never mind what's impossible," Curly Bill grumbled. "Just stick to the facts an'—"

49

"I'll conduct this inquiry, if it's all the same t' you," Butterball glowered, and banged Nick's bar again. You could almost see Nick wince when he hit it. "What would you give as the cause of Lou's death, Doc? You reckon this here knife of Marlatt's was the thing he was killed with?"

"Undoubtedly. From the position of the body I would say Mister Gromm was probably stooping over – perhaps intending to pull out a drawer of his desk, when Marlatt's knife was pl—"

"Would you say," Benton asked, "Lou had died right off?"

"I don't believe I'd care to say about that. Not, at any rate, without a post-mortem. He could have died very swiftly. On the other hand—"

"Look!" put in Curly Bill, exasperated. "I come here t' git some info'mation, friend. I didn't come here t' hear yo' head rattle. Did Lou kick the bucket right off or didn't he? Yes or no, now! I do' want no more jaw-waggin'!"

Doc Cranston peered across the rims of his spectacles. Then he dabbed at his face again; blew his nose vigorous.

"I don't know," he said.

Two or three of the tougher gents
50

snickered. But not very many, nor very damn long. Curly Bill Graham was no kind of fellow to do any laughing at. There was always the chance you might end up where Lou had gone.

But Curly Bill ignored them. He was right set on getting at the facts, seemed like. Him and Lou Gromm had been pretty thick.

"Don't know!" he said to Cranston. "What kinda sawbones are you anyhow? I'd sure hate t' trust a hoss t' you—"

The Doc, with his face a kind of stuck-pig color, said tartly: "Lou must have died within a minute or two!"

"Well, now," Bill said with a smile, "that's better. I give you back the witness, Butterball."

Frog sounds come out of Butterball's throat. He told the Doc that was all; called Cuervo.

It seemed like Cuervo was back in the bar again.

Butterball said, "Git up on this here soap box, Joe, an' tell these folks how you found Lou's body. An' let's not hev no more interruptions," he said for Curly Bill's benefit. "Go ahead, Joe."

Cuervo hitched up his cartridge belt and

let the crowd have a look at his teeth.

Butterball said to sort of set him off, "You sleep in that shack next the jailhouse, don't you?"

"*Si, señor* – with the Señor Flash Marlatt."

"Ah, yes. Uh – What time'd you come home? Las' night, I mean. S'pose you tell us all about it – about findin' Lou's body. Just give it to us in your own words, Joe."

Cuervo just grinned. He rolled his eyes at one of the floozies.

Butterball banged on the bar with his bung-starter. "Did you sleep at home las' night?"

"No, señor. I was make fiesta by Chato Bandera—"

"Ummm . . . yes. Come on now, Joe. Tell us all about it."

Cuervo preened his little black mustache. "I'm mebbe leave the fiesta leetle beet after two, señor. As I come past the marshal's office I'm try for light me the smoke. But no got tobacco. I'm see the light in the office. I'm think mebbeso the Señor Flash she's 'ave some—"

"So you stopped at the office. You supposed, of course, Marlatt was still on duty?"

"But yes, señor."

"Tell the boys what you found when you went into the office."

"I go eento the office. *Sangre de cristo!* I'm jomp like the rabbit! The Señor Flash, she's no dere. But the Señor Lou, she's dere weeth the face on desk—"

"Dead, eh?" Curly Bill questioned.

"But yes, señor."

Cuervo rolled his brown eyes wildly. "I'm see the blood on floor – the knife een hees back. She's mus' be dead. She's no get op an' walk!"

"Then you hustled over to Smith's an' woke up Marlatt, eh?"

"Si!"

Cuervo's nod was eager. "I'm wake Flash op an' she's say 'W'at's wrong' an' I'm say, 'The Señor Lou, she's dead lak' 'erring and we're go—"

"Yeah," muttered Curly Bill testily, "you went over to the office. Go on from there an' shake it up a little, will you?"

You could hear Butterball sigh clear across the bar room. "Honest, Bill, this job's hard enough – Oh, well! G'wan, Joe. You went over to the office—"

"If he goes over to the office again I'll scream!"

That was Curly Bill, of course; but he

53

didn't much look like he was thinking of screaming.

Cuervo swallowed his Adam's apple hurriedly, wiped the sweat off his face and gulped: "Flash, she's look at the Señor Lou an' hees face she's get white lak' the chalk een the schoolhouse. She's say—"

"Wait just a second," cut in Butterball Benton. "There's a point I'd like to get clear here first. Some of the boys on this jury ain't never been in that jail. They oughta be told a little somethin' about it. I think it should be mentioned that the cell walls is plumb solid an' the doors is made of inch iron bars. They've got new spring locks to 'em which can't noways be opened without you got the keys. There's just two sets of them keys. Lou packed one an' whoever was jailer usually packed the other."

He looked at the fellows who'd come up for jury duty like he wanted to make sure they'd got all that. Then his blue knobs of eyes swung round to Cuervo. "You was jailer yestidy afternoon, Joe. Still got your keys, ain't you?"

"But no—" Cuervo stared. "I'm geef them to Flash w'en I'm go to fiesta."

"Oh. Well, jus' so it's straight for the record. When you woke Flash, las' night, did he go for the Doc right off?"

"Een a minute, sure. But first she's say—"

Butterball said, "An' rightly, too. But you jus' hang hold of that a second, Joe. I wanta go back a mite so's these boys'll get the right picture. When you went into the office from the jail right after them miners left yestiday, I mean, what was it you told the Marshal?"

Cuervo waggled his eyes and crossed himself. "I'm tell the trut'. I'm say to the Señor Lou, 'Thees hombre, Cherokee Jack, she's say eef ever she's get loose of thees jail she's goin' for keel you sure.' "

"Right." Butterball looked pretty pleased with himself. "What was it, now, Flash said before he went after Doc Cranston?"

"She's say, 'Joe, you go take the look at them pris'ners.' "

"An' did you?"

"Sure. That Cherokee Jack she's not dere no more!"

Chapter Four

Fine Words From A Lawyer

YOU had to hand it to Butterball. Best dang coroner the town ever had. He sure knew how to keep a jury from sleeping.

There was more damn noise in Nick's bar room than hell emigrating on cart wheels. You never heard such a hullabaloo since Jim Wolf caught the tramp in his house. Everyone's jaw got to wagging at once and Butterball dang nigh ruint Nick's bar before he could make himself heard again.

For my part I'd heard aplenty. I'd of climbed out of there like a Neuches steer if there'd been any way I could *get* out. But there wasn't. I was right up front. I had no more chance than a wax cat in the hot place. I'd of been plumb willing to give up ten years of life if I could of seen what was coming when I let Jack out.

It looked a heap like I'd give them up anyway.

Butterball shouted: "Quiet! Shut up, you fellas, or I'll finish this private!"

It did quiet down a little.

I figured it was dollars to doughnuts he would call me next.

But he didn't.

He was all done calling.

He said, to all of us of course – but mostly to them horse thiefs alongside the bar: "I reckon that'll be about all, gents. You've heard all you need to listen at. Keepin' in mind it is your duty to determine from the evidence presented whether Lou Gromm died of a felony, a suicide or accident, you can now retire an' cook up a just an' true verdick.

"Oh – an' one other thing. If it should be your notion deceased an' his death come together of a felony, it's clearly within your means an' privilege to establish, if you can, the identity of Lou's killer."

He gave them a smile and a pat on the back. "That's all, boys. Hop to it."

The bar room buzzed like a pestered sidewinder. Some of that crowd was even laying their bets on which it would be – me, or Cherokee Jack Rogers.

Not that I was paying much notice.

I had plenty to figure on my ownself.

I felt like I'd come to the end of my rope. And the hell of it was, all I'd really done was to try and save that drunk old derelict from getting strung up for something he'd been too drunk to do if he'd wanted to.

Casting back over my acts it seemed like the future had got considerable foggy. Only one hunk of sunshine could I see in it any place. I had hung Cuervo's keys in the office.

Cuervo'd tossed me them keys when he went off at six. I had gone inside the office then and Lou had told me to take the night off . . . That he wasn't going to Tombstone, noways.

I had gone across to Doaks' stable then and had rented a horse. I had ought to of got out my own, of course, but my mind had been too fuzzed, I guess. Doaks had asked me where I was off to and I'd allowed I was going to the Cherrycow; which I hadn't, of course. I had rode through the hills thinking about Lou Gromm and them miners. And about what Tiltpot James had told Lou. And about where all this was like to wind up at. And, of course, I'd got thinking of Cherokee Jack, and of the fine raw deal Lou was fixing to hand him.

And then I'd come back to town. And left Doaks' bronc out in back of the office. And had gone inside and found the place empty.

That was when it had come to me what a first-class joke it would be on Lou if somebody up and let Cherokee Jack out.

Reckon I had ought to been bored for the simples.

I had put the plan into practise right pronto.

Just like a halfwit I had strolled down the corridor and into the jail room. Things had looked peaceful as two six-shooters in the same belt. That drifter, Roach, had had his face to the wall and was sawing off logs like a damn steam boiler. I'd gone catfooting back and had let Jack out. Roach was still snoring when we'd tiptoed past him.

I had let Jack out through the jail's back door. I had helped him up on Doaks' horse and told him: "You roll your hocks for the Border, Jack, an' don't come back or they'll hang you."

I had gone in then and locked the back door. I had hung Cuervo's keys on the nail by Lou's desk. After which, feeling downright good, I had gone on over to Jack Dall's for a drink.

I had sure laid up a pile of grief for myself!

It had been 9:35 when I let Cherokee loose. It was just about ten, when, wondering if Lou had discovered the jailbreak, I had gone back over and found Lou at his desk. He'd been busy sorting over the last of his mail which had come in on the late Tombstone stage.

He'd said, glancing up kind of wry like and sour, "S'posed you'd be takin' in the fiesta, Marlatt."

"Not me," I said. "I get enough Mex society round this office."

I tipped me a chair back against the wall and we'd indulged in some bull and small talk, me doing most of it and Lou just grunting.

Seemed like he was trying to shut me off some way. I guessed he was anxious to read through his letters. I seen there was three-four mebbe which he hadn't opened.

So I picked up the *Tombstone Epitaph* and pawed my way through its pages. Nothing like paper news to improve a guy's mind, I said.

Every so often I would sneak me a look at Lou. You could see all right he hadn't missed Jack none. He was humped by his desk smirking over his letters; only, once or twice, I caught him scowling. Which reminded me there'd been a peck of dames in Lou's life. And there was probably two or three, I reckoned, which hadn't proper taken to Lou's kind of treatment.

I sat there reading till pretty near twelve.

I was just fixing to leave when I recollected we still had Roach, that mirror-breaking drifter, locked up.

I asked Lou if he'd loosed Roach yet, but he didn't pay no attention. I said, "Mebbe you ought to – he's supposed to of been let out today."

But Lou never batted a eyelash. Them letters sure must of been interesting.

I give him a shrug and went home to bed.

It had been 2:15 when Cuervo woke me and give me a jolt with the news of Lou's stabbing. Right then was the first I had give any thought to what Cuervo had claimed Cherokee Jack aimed to do if ever he got himself out of Lou's jail.

I sweat aplenty as we hustled over.

There was Lou, all right. Just like Cuervo had said. With his face on the desk and my knife in his back.

I tried to remember where I'd left that knife. Near as I could tell it had been on Lou's desk. Seemed like I remembered him using it to open his letters.

I went over that office like a dog hunting fleas – made Cuervo look, too. But we didn't find nothing. Nothing, I mean, in the way of clues.

There wasn't so much as the least thing out of order.

Everything looked like it had at twelve. Except that Lou was dead with my knife in his back. There wasn't none of them 'clues' you hear about whatever. No loose heels off the culprit's boots. No dropped gloves nor women's handkerchiefs with initials neat done in their corners to help you. No quirts or spurs – no conchas come off the damn killer's chaps.

There was just dead Lou.

Dead Lou and my knife.

I sent Cuervo off to the cells to check up.

Course I knew mighty well what he'd find back there.

And he did. He found that Cherokee had slipped his moorings.

He come rushing back all white and shaking – as near white, leastways, as a Mex can look. You'd think the fool didn't trust his eyes, he was that shook up. But he managed to tell me Cherokee Jack had made good, had got himself loose and had killed Lou Gromm.

I was more than a little inclined to agree with him. I'd of bet my last nickel he hadn't killed Cramp Leyholt; but it sure looked like he had killed Lou Gromm.

Gratitude, I thought, has sure got a lot of funny kinks in its tail! A fine way Jack had taken to repay my favor!

I got to thinking then about testimony given at Leyholt's inquest. It had been showed mighty plain there'd been bad blood between them – between Cramp Leyholt and Cherokee. They had argued over a poker game the night before in Jack Dall's saloon. Cherokee had called Cramp a lot of hard names no man would take unless his wife had flung them. Cramp wasn't no guy to call hard names at. He had laid the old drunk out cold as a cucumber. Then he'd picked up Cherokee and heaved him out in the gutter.

All this was Hack Averill's testimony.

Hack was a blackleg lawyer from Fort Huachuca.

Tilt James had drove up outside just as Cherokee got up from the gutter. According to Tilt, Cherokee had got up and shaken his fist at Dall's batwings and had sworn bloody murder he'd get even with Cramp.

Hack Averill had found Cramp's body in the alley between Jack Dall's and the stage office. That was the night the stage company's safe had been looted of $2,500 – hard money. Though they hadn't found *that* out till later. When the agent opened up next morning.

It looked, right enough, like Jack was a hard case proper – though, up till now, I hadn't believed it.

Now, I wasn't none too sure. He could of easy come back last night, after I'd turned him loose, and snuffed Lou's light.

Trouble was if he *had*, he had sure enough taken one ripsnorting way of repaying the favor I'd done him!

It was the stage company's contention he had robbed their safe; that, some way, Leyholt had caught him at it and Jack had killed Leyholt to shut his mouth.

Which was plausible enough, but hardly convincing – special if you knew Cherokee Jack Rogers like I did. He hadn't the character for that sort of thing. It just wasn't in the cards, I thought. He *did* run off at the mouth too much; made a heap of wild brags and predictions. But the dang fool was drunk two-thirds of the time. Rest of the time he was sleeping.

Still, I thought, he might of done it. He *might* of killed Lou just like Hack had claimed . . .

The jury tramped out of Nick's back room and lined themselves up by the bar. They wore a kind of strained, solemn look, like a tenderfoot trapper skinning a skunk.

The foreman, Hack Averill, cleared his throat.

He said without wasting none of Curly Bill's time: "We've decided, Butterball, that Lou Gromm's death was a felony. That he was killed in cold blood by Cherokee Jack, with the aid an' connivance of Marlatt's knife. An' it's our considered opinion . . . our opinion," he said – and I saw the faint sneer that was curling his mouth, "that the aforesaid deputy, Flash Marlatt, be real careful looked into . . . Mister Marlatt's activities last evenin', that is."

Chapter Five

"*Thinkin'*
*Won't Git You
Out Of It*"

IT could of been worse. It could of been a whole lot worse.

65

I was kind of surprised it hadn't been.

A feud had been cooking between Hack Averill and me for the past two weeks – ever since, to put it right down in the record, I'd got wise he cottoned to Dora James and was making elephant tracks around her.

Course it's true Dora and me didn't have no 'understanding'. I hadn't no holds on her noways. But everyone knew I was sparking her, and had steered their looks elsewhere, according. I'd been setting the bag ever since I showed up there, and I wasn't figuring nohow on having to share the business with no damn tinhorn from Huachuca.

I had gone to Averill's office, a little old two-by-four cubbyhole he had up over the butcher shop, and had politely unravelled my sentiments. But Averill was one of them hombres that can't never take a decent hint to him noways.

So I put it plain.

I said, "Don't go botherin' around over at Dora's no more, Hack. Just keep yourself plumb away from her or you an' me's due to tangle."

And he said, kind of sneering like: "Just what're you allowin' to do about it, mister?"

I didn't beat around no bushes. I said, "Keep on, by grab, an' you'll sure find out"; and when he folded up his dukes I popped him. I knocked him all the way down them damn narrow stairs and he was still counting stars when I left him.

I'd supposed that had ought to settle it. But it begun to look now like it hadn't.

I was wondering what I'd better do when Weak Back sloshed himself into the office. He slammed down his hat with an oath.

"By cripes!" he said, "you'll be saucered an' blowed like a cup of over-boiled cawfee! Any guy which ain't got—"

"What are you brewin' about?"

" 'Bout *you!*" he snapped. "An' Lou Gromm's killin'! 'F you was so all-fired lathered t' git him kilt off—"

"Now just a minute," I cut in a mite peeved-like. "You better get this straight. I never killed Lou. I didn't plan to kill him. Nor I wasn't figurin' to get him killed – not that he wasn't deservin' it, though."

We eyed each other like a couple mad bulls.

Then I said, "I admit I let Jack out – prob'ly do it again if the deal shaped that way. He no more killed Cramp Leyholt than *you* did! D'you reckon he'd of quarreled with Leyholt if he'd had it in mind to kill him? Or if he hadn't been piped to the gills?

67

Why, he – Dammit," I said, "if Cramp—"

"I dunno about Cramp," Weak Back grunted, "but he sure as hell killed Lou, all right. He said he would, an' he did, by grab! An' look what a fine stew *you* jumped into! Y' orta knowed Hack Averill'd be layin' for you! Look what he—"

"Never mind Hack. I let Cherokee loose about quarter to ten. You heard what the Doc told that jury – said Lou'd been stabbed around twelve o'clock. You reckon Jack hung around waitin' all that time? You take him for a plain damn nitwit? By the time Lou was killed Jack ought to of been a mighty far piece towards the Border."

"If he went," Weak Back said; and snorted. "You're a sight too chicken-hearted t' be packin' the law in a camp like this. What's the difference to you if Cherokee swings fer Cramp's killin'? He ain't never advantaged *you* none that I've heard of."

"Never mind," I said. "Right's right an' wrong's wrong—"

"Ahr – you an' yer copybook – Say!" he exclaimed, suddenly snapping his fingers. "By cripes!" he said. "Do you know . . . Hack *could* of done it—"

"Done what?" I said. "You mean Hack Averill?"

Weak Back nodded as though to his thinking. "Yes, sir," he grunted. "Hack sure could of done it, all right . . ."

"You mean killed *Lou?*"

Weak Back nodded. "What in the Seven Hinges for?" I said.

"How do *I* know what for? Lotsa things Hack mighta done it for. Ain't you never heard what Lou done t' Hack over at Charleston las' year when Lou was J.P.? Y'aint? Hell! Hack had just come down from Huachuca then – the Colonel had drove him out fer peddlin' stuff t' them Injuns over there. Hack rode into Charleston one afternoon feelin' chipper as three larks, account of he'd just made a deal t' git into the cow business. Y'd of thought, t' hear the way his jaw was waggin', he was a secon' John Chisum. He was aimin' t' celebrate, an' he sure done it! Liked t' turned that town upside down! He was just windin' up fer the oncore, as the fella says, when Lou come larrupin' up in a lather. Lou never said a word – jest retched out his hand an' drug that pore deluded Hack Averill plumb outa the saddle. An' what I mean is he *drug* 'im! Hack opened his jaw to say a few things an' Lou cuffed him a couple between the horns that would of

69

stopped most anything short of a cyclone. It sure stopped Hack, I'm here t' tell you. Lou socked him one so hard on the jaw Hack could scratch his back with his front teeth, almost. An' when they brought Hack to again, Lou fined him twenty-three hundred head of prime beef – every last critter Hack had to his name. He hadn't never got no land nor no buildin's. Just them cattle an' a couple tough hands he had hired off John Slaughter who was on his way no'th to the high grass lands of Wyomin'. Lou made Hack write him out a bill of sale fer 'em before he would let Hack loose. Then—"

"Well," I said, thinking it over, "mebbe Hack *did* have some cause . . ." A lot of guys, I knew, would kill a man for less. And Hack might of seen in the way things shaped up last night a chance to even two scores with one knife thrust. My score and Lou's.

"An' here's another thing," Weak Back muttered. "Ike Shotwell was sayin' somethin' about seein' Joe Cuervo up around this place last night. 'Long about twelve, too, 'cordin' to Ike's tell of it. I had t' do considerable arguin', but I finally got it out of him that Cuervo was actin' mighty sly an' suspicious. Ike claims Cuervo hung around

70

here in the shadders f'r upwards of twenty minutes; seemed to Ike like he was tryin' t' peer inside here at somethin'. Oh, well—if you ain't figurin' t' worry none over it, I don't see no reason why I sh'd git any gray hairs over it."

He shrugged Cramp Leyholt's troubles away; Lou Gromm's an' mine along with them. Then he seemed to recollect something and pulled a crumpled paper from his pocket. "Want t' hear m' new verses?" he inquired real modest, starting to get the paper opened up.

"Not now," I said. "I wanta do some thinkin'."

"The time to of thought was before you done it. Thinkin' won't git you outa it now. You better listen; *some* day folks is gonna pay real money for this—lemme read that las' verse first. You want t' git the sequench. Listen—

"He forked a wild mustang, a flea-bitten broncho,
  A bundle of skin that was wrapped in sho't hair—
Nose curved like a compass, his teeth was like shovels;
  His neigh was a blast like the snort of a bear.

"This flea-bitten cayuse was smart as ten dollars,
  Command from Ol' Jawbone he'd stan'
Parade Rest—
His legs was all spavined, his toes was like pigeons';
  At gallop his record was best in the West.

"A flick of the reins to the groun' an' he'd stan' there,
  A bottle of beer an' he'd stan' there all day—
He hated the rain an' the thunder an' lightnin';
  He turned his humped nose up at oats an' plain hay.

"He'd eat oysters in season an' sourdough an' tripe—"

He broke off sudden and stared at me funny.

"Say! Where'd you leave that hoss you got off Doaks? I damn near forgot t' tell you, but Doaks is spreadin' it all over town you rented a bronc las' night an' never brought it back. You never give him t' Cherokee, did you?"

72

I got out the makings and curled up a smoke. "I . . . uh – Well, I . . . just *lent* it to him, in a manner of speakin'."

"Jus' lent – *Great Caesar's pants!*" yowled Weak Back; and looked at me like I was some kind of freak. "My Gawd!" he said, and shook his head. "The things you don't think up t' do – you're worse'n my brother!" he snapped, disgusted. "You'll git no advantage outa *that*, I kin tell you! You're goin' t' be for it, surer'n shootin'; you've left a trail bigger'n ol' man Chisholm."

He took a turn with his hands in his pockets, then come back to stand and glower at me, nasty. He asked real soft and purry: "When y' took this famous ride las' night, did y' go on out to the Cherrycows like y' told Joe Doaks you aimed to? . . . Oh! Is that so? Well let me give you some advice, Mister Marlatt: Don't linger aroun' these hills no longer. Don't wait till night – don't wait fer nothin'. Jus' climb aboard of the first bronc y' find—"

"I ain't the kind that pulls for the tules," I said.

Weak Back eyed me a moment and snorted. Then he tapped his big rough hand on my shoulder. "You git on a hawss, boy,

73

an' git on quick. Git started right now or they'll hang you higher'n that smelter smokestack!"

Chapter Six

The Growl Of The Beast

"FOR what?" I said. "Not, by God, for Lou's killin', because they've already plastered Cherokee with that—"

"They kin dang well change their minds!" sniffed Weak Back. "You sh'd seen what happened t' my brother! They—"

His brother – which nobody believed he'd ever had any brother noways – had got to be an exasperation round the Galeyville marshal's office. He had used to bring his so-experienced brother into the talk every whipstitch till Lou Gromm got plumb fed up one day and told him to "for Chrissake forget the bastard, will you?"

I said as much myself, only politer. I said, "Never mind your brother – it's my neck that's on my mind right now."

Weak Back snorted and waggled his head

like a sawbones sage from the back of beyond. "You kin hang jest as high fer a sheep as a goat." And sniffed again for good measure.

"You got hangin' on the brain," I growled; and heaved my smoke through the window. A sound chopped short, like a stifled curse; and I jumped for a look, Weak Back right with me, yanking his gun as he stuck his head out.

But we didn't see nobody; just a shadowy shape off down towards the smelter that Weak Back decided must be Rube Haddon. I said, "Rube wouldn't of been snoopin' round listenin'."

"Don't seem so," Weak Back muttered; then drew in his breath like he'd bumped his belly against the snout of a sixgun or something. "Look! Looky there!"

I followed the look of his eyes and swore.

There was boot marks under the window.

We pulled in our heads real thoughtful. " 'Pears like somebody's a heap scared he might git t' miss somethin'. I recollect a certain party—"

"Too thin," I said. "Anybody might of made them tracks."

"*Might* of, yeah. But—"

"There's a lot of guys wears star plates on

75

their heels."

"But there ain't many wears such pointed ones," Weak Back said like that settled it. "Nor such pointed toes. The's just one gent wears that combination."

I knew who he meant. Jose Cuervo. Jose's boots would leave a track like that.

Not that I figured they had left it. If he wanted to hear what our talk was about, all he had to do was come in the office. "Somebody else," I said, "mighta been wearin' Joe's boots."

Weak Back give me a hard look and sniffed. "You sure got a mort o' Christian charity. If you go in fer preachin', leave me pass the hat."

I reckoned that was meant to be sarcasm.

I went over to Lou's desk and set down on it. I was pretty much worried in spite of my jaw wagging. Quite a heap could be made out of what I'd done, special if any guy had a reason for it. They could make me look like mud on a stick; and it began to look like they was trying to. If they was, there was just two reasons. Either someone was figuring to pay off a grudge, or the killer seen I was a first-class chance for him to get himself out of this jackpot. Or, I thought, both them reasons might be strung

76

right together.

I told Weak Back this idea.

Weak Back actually smiled when I told him. "Jus' what I been thinkin'," he said. "You know Joe Cuervo an' Hack's been real thick here late-like. Meetin' up at all kind of queer places. I come across em' down in the bottoms the other day. Down in the Turkey Creek bottoms, along near that ol' shack Jack Swartz built. I been wonderin' some what their idear was. They put up quite a show fer me – like the cat does after he's et the canary. But you could tell all right they'd been up to somethin'. An' knowin' Hack Averill, I – Say! has anyone let that drifter out yet?"

I'd clean forgot all about Ed Roach. He hadn't even had any breakfast, unless Joe Cuervo had gone and got it for him. "He'll be ringy," I said, "as a bear with his tail trapped."

We tramped on out to the jail room.

Sure enough, Roach was still locked up. He was stretched on his bunk with his face to the wall – just like he'd been last night when I saw him. Only, now, he didn't seem to be doing no snoring.

I said: "C'mon, fella. Rise an' shine! This here ain't no park. Git up and git a wiggle on."

Weak Back was over unlocking the door.

He swung it open. "This ain't no *ho-tel*," he told Roach; and the drifter turned over and heaved himself up, with a scowl and a curse, and put his still booted feet on the floor.

He sat there, watching us with his odd, yellow eyes.

"Where's my belongin's at?"

"You'll get them," I told him; and Weak Back said: "You hear any disturbance round here las' night? Damn funny! That other guy we had got away on us somehow. Seems like you ought to know somethin' about it."

"Well I don't," Roach scowled; and then yawned in our faces. "I slept straight through."

"All night?"

"No – I spent half the night tryin' to think up somethin' to write on your walls."

Weak Back peered round with a suspicious scowl.

But the guy was just being sarcastic; or, maybe, that was his idea of humor. He was a wild looking jasper with his uncut hair hanging near to his shoulders. It looked just now like the rats had slept in it, and his gray-streaked mustache stuck out every whichway. He rasped a scarred paw over his scraggle of whiskers and gave us a look from his pale, yellow eyes. With his whiney voice and meeching stare, his runover boots and his bony shoulders he looked like something the cat had dragged in. So far as plain looks went, I thought, there wasn't much choice between him and Cherokee. Just a couple old range bums down on their luck.

"Where you from?" I asked, to be sociable.

He never so much as give me a look. He lifted a paw to his beard-stubbled face again, made a vague motion like the kind them magicians make over their stovepipes.

But he didn't bring no rabbit out. He just kind of sighed like he'd lost his last friend. "I've shore seen a mort of jails in my day," he said, "but this here juzgado shore takes the medal. Where do you send fer your grub?" he asked Weak Back. "That egg your Mex brought me fer breakfast—"

"Never mind knockin' the chuck," Weak Back scowled. "We got things on our mind besides your eatin'. Marshal was killed las' night. You kill 'im?"

"Sure," Roach sneered. "I croaked him with one of these cell bars."

I said: "What did you bust McConaghey's

mirror for?"

"I couldn't tell if 'twas glass or Mex tin. I laid a bet with myself an' broke it to—"

"Oh, you did, did you?" Weak Back bristled. "Well, lemme tell you—"

"Save it fer them as appreciates wind. I've heard every tune you kind kin whistle an' I don't like none of 'em. That's the worst of these back-country coolers," he said; "y' gotta take s' much jaw from the sheriffs. Every John Law that gits a star pinned onto 'im—"

"If you don't hush up I'll pin a star on *you!*" snarled Weak Back, balling his fists up.

Roach cringed back, his show of bravado gone like slush in a Texas sun. He backed off like he thought Weak Back would really work him over a few; but his flat, yellow stare looked as mean as ever. I reckoned if he'd ever done much gambling that stare must of been a real asset to him. It was no help to me, any more than the rest of him. You just couldn't place him – couldn't figure him nohow. He was a regular sackful of contradictions. You couldn't even rightly tell what he looked like – I mean, what he *would* of looked like if he'd had a bushel of that hair cut off of him.

Spidery – that's the impression he give.

What part of his face showed above his whiskers was brown and creased as a left-out saddle. He was dressed like a miner, but that didn't prove nothing. The dirt on his clothes wasn't noways all mud. It was trail dust, a lot of it. Some of the trail grit still powdered his whiskers. He didn't look like he had ever washed; nor he didn't much smell like it, either. He had strong looking hands horned with callous and rope scars. His short, squatty legs showed the bow of a saddle. Which things might mean a lot, but probably meant nothing.

He was just a damned drifter. That was all you could say.

I said, "Okay," to Weak Back. "Give him his truck an'—"

"*Listen!*" hissed Weak Back, and held his left hand up.

I got a slice of it then and my blood run cold.

It was the voice of a mob.

"Out the back way – *quick!*" Weak Back shoved me. "Rustle, you fool! Grab a bronc an' git goin!"

Chapter Seven

Off Like A Pot Leg

THEM was fine large days we had back in Galeyville. Fine to look back on. Fine to remember. Days bright with sunshine, with life and with laughter. Thrill spiced days steeped with hell, with adventure. There was something doing every minute of the day; and the nights were raucous, gilded red with the flares of the miners' campfires. The sough of the wind through the pines was a melody frequent flung down from the towering Cherrycows, and the sharp, flat bark of a rifle or belt gun was nothing at all to get your sweat up about – not, I mean to say, unless its lead was heaved at you.

I could take my chances with plain gray lead. But being framed up for a whole town's scapegoat, I told myself, was something I hadn't bargained for when I pinned Lou Gromm's tin star on my shirt.

I had reckoned, up till now, I could bluff it out. But now I knew better. I was picked for the booby.

A mob ain't no thing to be shouting 'Boo!' at.

I caught at the keys I saw Weak Back

chuck me. Clacked one into the lock – tore the door open. I went banging my boots through the back yard's tin cans. But the racket was feeble compared to that mob's sound. Three or four voices rose plain and clear. It was Curly Bill's shout jumped new speed to my sprinting.

"Open up!" he was yowling. "We're after Flash Marlatt – an' what I mean, we air goin' to git him!"

There was a loose-coupled roan tied out back of McConaghey's. I piled into the saddle without no scruples. With a mob at your bootheels you ain't got much time to be thinking which is the right thing or which is the wrong. The horse wasn't mine but I took him – immediate. I jerked the reins loose and brought them down on his tail end pronto. He jumped like a fire had been lighted under him.

But halfway out of town I got thinking. I sawed on the reins and pulled up short. I slammed the roan towards Hack Averill's office. It was over the butcher shop next to Ike Shotwell's.

A damn fool play. Ain't no doubt about it.

I was crazy mad at the way things was shaping and it had got in my mind it might be Hack Averill framing me so's to get him a clear inside track with Dora. If it was, by gee, I would wring the truth out of him!

And there was always the chance, remembering Weak Back's story, he had killed Lou his ownself.

I was in a mood to believe it.

I went up Hack's stairs three steps to the jump. I damn near yanked the door from its hinges. But Hack wasn't there. The place was plumb empty.

I come out and, with a curse for my luck, realized Bill's crowd had seen me. Lead splattered the steps with splinters off the railing; pounded the boards at my back like hailstones. It got plain I had better get off them stairs pronto.

A slug jerked my vest – another cuffed my hatbrim.

The ground rushed up as I jumped from the stairs. I staggered three steps and clawed into the saddle.

I jammed my steel hard into that bronc and he rocketed off like a sledge had struck him. Aiming for Doaks' place I looked over my shoulder.

What I could see wasn't no nerve tonic.

They was coming all right. They was coming like hornets. I could see Curly Bill

dashing after his horse, and Jaw Bone Clark
going down on one knee with his cheek to a
rifle.

I heard his first whistler bite high past my
shoulder and then I was rounding the T.P.
Bar and for some twenty seconds was out of
their seeing.

We tore down a alley.

We come up behind Joe Doaks' corral.

Joe saw me coming and clawed for a
cloud.

"I – I – I was on'y funnin', Flash – hones'
t' Gawd I was! I n-n-never meant—"

"To hell with your meant," I said.
"Where's Averill's horse?"

"He – he took it . . ."

"When? Where?" I barked frantic.

Doaks pointed a shaking hand at the hills.
At the dark, rimming ridge crest off towards
the San Simon.

I jabbed in my spurs. There was just one
thing for it.

Hack Averill had gone to the Cherrycow
outfit.

I seen quick enough *I* wasn't going out
there. I'd lost too much time fogging round
at Hack Averill's. It looked like being nip
and tuck if I got away from that mob at all.

I've heard plenty talk about a 'officer's duty' – Lou Gromm was always feeding it at us – him that was practically Curly Bill's pardner. But I ain't no Wyatt Earp, nor I wasn't craving to be. Angel wings is all right, I guess; but I sure wasn't hankering to have none pinned on me. I crowded that bronc what you'd call 'tall, wide and handsome'.

And felt no shame for it, neither.

Curly Bill, and them fellows with him, was some of the saltiest bucks in that whole stretch of country. They was considered, at this time, the scourge of the Arizona ranges, not confining their devilment just to the Cherrycows, but working clean over into Grant County, New Mexico, and south well into Sonora. And there wasn't nothing tinhorn about the brand of hell they raised. They tackled just about everything and did a good solid business in cattle, besides – other folks' cattle, to be real exact. There was scads and scads of whopping big longhorns grazing the pastures of Sonora and Chihuahua, so many thousands their owners never even bothered taking tally. Curly did a wholesale business with these critters, turning them over at a good fat profit to the contractors supplying the Injuns with beef. A few of his markets shipped the steers East or disposed of them to a number of local slaughterhouses who weren't too particular where their beef come from.

Curly Bill seldom rode without he made a good profit. He didn't see no use going after them Mexican cattle empty-handed. From the local ranchers in the San Simon and San Pedro valleys – even over into the Sulphur Springs Valley, he would gather up stock for the Mexican markets; and as a kind of sideline to this end of his trade he would run off horses from the undermanned army posts. I've heard it said his activities was even discussed by Congress.

He had another good business that paid him well. From the Animas Valley, away over in New Mexico, there is a trail winds down through the towering Peloncillos to the San Simon Valley. This trail was known as Skeleton Canyon – and damn well named, you can bet on that! Mex smugglers used it on their way to Tucson, driving their mules heavy laden with silver. For a while Curly Bill used to wipe them out regular, but it finally got so the smugglers quit coming. There ain't many Mexes like a no-return trail, and this one got practically paved with their bones.

I didn't know how bad Curly Bill wanted

to come up with me, and I didn't wait around none to find out, neither. Looking across my shoulder I could see quite a passel of his toughest bucks in that bunch; Joe Hill, Sandy King, Jim Hughes, Tom McLowery, John Ringo and a couple of the Clantons, not to mention all the half baked outlaws that was tagging after them – Pete Spence, Russian Bill, Zwing Hunt, Billy Grounds and others of like kidney. Curly Bill and Lou Gromm had been thicker than gar soup thickened with tadpoles and if he figured it was Cherokee had murdered Lou Gromm, and got it in his head I had helped Cherokee flit, the best thing I could do was keep right on going.

Which was what I aimed to do.

I had lined out hoping to cut the Tombstone road, knowing Curly Bill's crowd would never follow me there, because if there was any one thing Curly couldn't abide it was Wyatt Earp and his hell-roaring kin. But I could see pretty quick I would have my work cut out if I tried to make Tombstone on *that* nag. He didn't have no more bottom than a brand new sieve.

He give all he had to give – Curly Bill's blue whistlers took care of that; but unless I could get me another horse quick it would be all over with me but the spade work.

That was when I see the guy jogging ahead of me.

He was quite a piece off but he heard the commotion. I seen him look around and I said "Halleluya!" It was Jack McCann on his thoroughbred filly, Molly McCarthy – as fast a mare as there was in the country.

He seen what was up and he come a-scouting.

" 'Tis kind av warmish fer racin', lad."

"Hell's warmer!" I said. "Lemme take your mare, will you?"

McCann squinted round at the larruping outlaws. You couldn't mistake Curly Bill in the lead. And McCann, I knew, was friendly with Bill. "A bit av a misunderstandin' ye've bin havin', is it?"

"Yeah," I said. "He'll be all right when he's got time to think it over, but right now he's madder than a centipede with chilblains."

"Thin take Molly an' welcome—"

I was onto the mare before he'd done talking; and it wasn't long before the Galeyville mob was a dwindling dust in the heat-hazed distance.

Chapter Eight

Jack McCann's Mare

I HADN'T rode so terrible far till I got to thinking about Hack Averill again who, surer than sin, had gone out to the Cherry-cow. I didn't have to guess what he'd gone out there for. He'd gone to see Dora, and there wasn't no telling what a pussy-faced skunk like him would think up to tell her. He was figuring, I reckoned, to put a spoke in my wheel.

I turned in the saddle and took a squint at my back trail.

I couldn't see no more dust.

So I pulled Miz' McCarthy down to a walk.

I had come quite a ways in the wrong direction – wrong, I mean, considering my thoughts of the Cherrycow. But that could be remedied. By quitting the trails and going through the mesquite brush I could still make the James' spread by noontime tomorrow. By then, like enough, Hack Averill would be on his way back to town and I could find out from Dora what the hell he'd been up to.

Be a longish ride between meals, looked

like, but I guessed I could do it; and I figured I ought to. So I pulled Miz' Molly McCarthy around and headed her south by east through the mountains. She might get clawed up by the brush a little, but I guessed it wouldn't hurt her if we took it easy.

She was a joy to ride. It was just like sitting in a low-back rocker. She was a slim and mighty plucky old girl and her shoulder muscles rippled like a wind in velvet.

But there was a deal too much buzzing round in my head for me to give much note to the horse I was riding. I guessed Hack Averill had gone to the Cherrycow to tell Dora the law was hunting me for rubbing Lou Gromm out.

It wasn't, of course – there wasn't nobody hunting me but Curly Bill's outlaws, and they had likely quit by this time. But it wouldn't be long before the law *was* hunting me. Joe Doaks and the rest would be seeing to that.

Doaks and me never had hit it off. He was an undersized shrimp with ears like a mule and a nose like a rabbit – always twitching and always sniffing out trouble; and he'd poked it into my business before. Only reason I kept my horse at his place was because there wasn't no other livery in town.

The more I thought about the mess I'd got into, the worse my future prospects looked. I could of left the country, of course. But I wouldn't. Not while Hack Averill was free to spark Dora. Not by a jugful!

But I couldn't of been much worse off if I'd actually been the guy that killed Lou Gromm. Everything I'd done seemed to shove me in deeper. The quicker I got hold of Hack Averill – or Joe Cuervo, one, the sooner I'd get to the truth of what happened. I would of bet my bottom dollar on that. Joe Cuervo and Averill had been cooking up something or they'd not have been meeting places like Weak Back had said they was.

I got so busy thinking about them and about what I would do to Hack Averill, I forgot all about Tilt James' prediction. I guessed Hack must of got a lot of laughs over the way I'd involved myself in Lou's killing.

It was plain enough now, I thought, how they'd worked it.

Cuervo had come snooping around and, quick as the coast was clear, he'd give Hack the high sign. Then Hack had snuck in and let Lou have it – had my knife, I mean. Right between Lou's shoulders. It must have pleasured him plenty to find my knife so damn handy.

It was pretty near dark when I come onto Chandler's ranch.

The house stood dark and silent. I had met its owner a number of times and hadn't been much impressed. He kept a few dairy cows and some way made a living off them. His place was near Antelope Springs on the road between Tombstone and the Cherry-cows, and was a favourite stopping place for lumber freighters; it was even more highly thought of by the owlhooter breed who stopped by frequent on their trips between Tombstone and Galeyville. It had been originally owned by a jasper called Stockton Edmunds, who had got his monicker as one of the few survivors from the Stockton Indian massacre a number of years back. I wasn't sure, but I had a sort of halfway hunch that Chandler, the present owner, was more than a little bit friendly with Curly Bill and his hardcase riders.

Like I say, the house was dark. There wasn't no sign of anyone being round. I didn't know if I would be smart to stop.

The lack of light and activity might well be a blind to things Mister Chandler didn't want advertised. There might, I thought, be some unfriendly jaspers looking me over from back of those oak trees flanking Shoot-'Em-Up Creek, or from back of the wood pile's dark shape yonder. It might, I thought, be smarter to go hungry.

I decided to chance it.

When I'd got to within a hundred yards of the creek where, flanked by the trees, it flowed past the front door, I raised me a shout.

"You home there, Chandler?"

There wasn't no answer for perhaps twenty seconds, then a dark shape moved from the gloom of the oak trees.

It was Chandler. There was a rifle slung careless in the crook of his arm. I could see three-four more shapes shift weight by the creekbank.

Chandler gruffed something I couldn't quite catch. Then he came a bit nearer. "Who's talkin'?" he grunted.

"Marlatt," I said. "Deputy marshal at Galeyville. Why all the caution?"

"Well, you can't never tell. It don't pay to git careless – not in this man's country. Coley Finley damn near took lead poisonin' steppin' out this way the other night. There's a lot of tough jaspers driftin' through these hills. Thought at first you was mebbe that damn rapscallion, Curly Bill. By yourself, are you?"

"Just me an' sweet Molly McCarthy," I said.

"What the hell you doin' on Molly, Marlatt? You ain't turned horse thief, hev you?"

"Humor's wasted on a hungry man, Chandler. I'm huntin' Cherokee Jack Rogers. Ain't seen him, have you? He broke jail last night."

"No," Chandler said; then snorted. "I thought that jail was s'posed to be foolproof."

"S'posin's one thing. Facts is somethin' else. Got anything warmin' on the back of the stove? I ain't et since mornin'."

Chandler seemed to be thinking it over. I seen one of the shapes by the creek shift his rifle.

"Might be a little sowbelly an' beans left. Light an' share it . . . if you don't mind takin' it from the wife an' kids."

I looked at them guys by the creek again.

"I guess I ain't that hungry," I said.

I camped about eight miles farther on.

Didn't make no fire. I give Molly a couple hours' rest and pushed on again, taking it slow. I might be wrong, but it looked a heap like, to me, Jack Chandler was having truck with gents he'd ought to steer plumb clear of. Though it might just be he couldn't help himself. Curly Bill's gang had ways of persuasion.

I remembered the time Bill and some of his men was having a poker game over at Fort Thomas and Old Man Lloyd come busting in on his horse, drunker than three fiddlers. It was in a saloon owned by a fellow named Mann. I guess old Lloyd thought to play a joke on his friends. Anyway, he come in on his horse – or, to be strictly truthful, on Joe Hill's horse. Hill being a Curly Bill man and one of the card players. Lloyd's gun shots got themselves a chorus pronto. Hill's horse went out with an empty saddle. Lloyd stayed where he'd fallen, riddled, on the floor. The card game went on without further interruption. "No better hand," Curley Bill said, throwing in his discard, "ever punched cows than Ol' Lloyd. Nice ol' codger. I'll take two, Joe – gimme aces."

But I didn't think about Curly Bill long; nor Chandler, neither. I had things a heap more important on my mind – more important to me. Mostly, I thought of Hack Averill and Cuervo. I guessed I'd arrest Hack quick as I saw him. I'd find some way to have the whole truth out of him if I had to beat him within a inch of his life. This brotherly love stuff is all well and good. If it's generally practised. When it ain't you got to use something more potent. I figured to use something more potent on Hack.

Hack's past acts as I knew them didn't recommend him to charity. He was a diamondback rattler in a bull snake's clothing. A tinhorn lawyer who'd steal your eyeteeth out of you, and then charge you extra for the work it made him. I knew at least three widows the snake had foreclosed on.

I'd drag him back to town and work him over proper. If he didn't kick in I would work some on Cuervo. That dang sly Mex was slicker than splatter.

I guessed I could get the truth out of one of them.

About Lou Gromm – about Lou's killing, I mean.

It was along about noon when I got to the Cherrycow. The whole and right name of James' spread was the Chiricahua Land and Cattle Company, but the Texans who made

97

up most of the outfit couldn't demean themselves by saying anything as fancy as that so they called James' spread the Cherrycow outfit. And everyone else done the same.

Like I said, it was most near noon when I got there, and by that time my plans for Hack was coming six to the minute. But, as things turned out, they was a little pree machoor.

Because Hack wasn't there.

He had been there and gone.

But Tilt James was there – handy as a kitchen sink. Though all that I seen first off was Dora.

She was standing in the shade of the wide veranda. She was eying me odd-like, kind of frosty and hostile. Her eyes had a glint like sun off a bottle.

I hooked me a leg around Molly's saddle horn.

It looked like if there was going to be any chin music heard I was going to be the one to furnish it.

I said, tentative like, "What have I gone an' done *this* time?"

"Done!" she said. "You know mighty well what you've done, Flash Marlatt! Oh! – how can you sit there so brazen after—"

"*I*'ll tend to that fella!" Tilt James' voice

bellowed.

I whirled like a scorpion had got up my pants leg.

There he was, looking mean and ugly. Not twenty yards off. By the pole corral, with a .45-90 cocked and clapped to his shoulder.

I didn't wait to see if he'd fire.

I remembered right sudden what he'd told me in town – what he'd told me would happen if I brought myself out here.

In that split second I thought of a heap of things I'd of been better off if I'd thought of sooner.

Tiltpot James had an uncaring temper. Get up his mad and he'd just as lief shoot as spit – maybe liefer. And right now he was mad enough to bust his nut-crackers.

He meant business. He showed it. He had a eagle eye squinching down his gun sights when I plastered myself to Miz' McCarthy's off side and took to the timber like hell a-whooping. How he ever missed is God's own mercy – might be account of he was so furious mad; but he creased my saddle twice with his lead. Molly laid back her ears and plain bolted. She forgot all her miseries when Tilt's lead started screaming. She *ran*.

Chain lightning hung fire by comparison.

Chapter Nine

"Grab A Hawss An' Git Goin'!"

THE supper fires was burning bright when I got my next glimpse of Galeyville. My gut felt gant as the eye of a needle but I hadn't no time to be feeding it.

I got the word at the edge of town.

Ike Shotwell hailed me, waving frantic.

Good sort, Ike. Run the general store, he did, and done his best to keep on terms with the entire population.

"Turn around!" he cried. "Wheel that bronc an'—"

"Look again," I said. "This ain't no bronc. This here's a lady. Miz' Molly McCarthy – pride an' fortune of—"

"Never mind that! You wheel her an' git!"

"What's itchin' you?" I said and, reaching down, caught a hold of his shoulder. "I'm a hungry man, Ike. Why should I—"

"My soul above!" Ike howled. "Ain't you *heard?*"

"Heard what?"

"My Gawd!" Ike said. "You've just come back from the Cherrycow, ain't you?"

"Yes," I said, "an'—"

"That drifter, Roach, found Hack Averill out on that trail with a hole in his chest you could drive a six-horse hitch through!"

It was plain, I seen, that events didn't wait on no man.

I shook off Ike's hand. I got out of the saddle and tossed him the reins. "Hold Molly," I said, and rolled my hocks for the marshal's office by way of the nearest can-littered alley.

I made a heap more racket than I aimed to, but I hadn't no time to be choosy. I had to see Weak Back pronto. I aimed to get at the facts of this business, and I guess you could of heard me all over town the way I banged on the jail's back door.

Weak Back opened it, blinked and swore.

Then he grabbed my arm and yanked me in. "Damned," he said, "if you don't take the medal. Ain't you got no—"

I said, "Never mind that. Just give me the facts on this Averill killin'. Where's that sawed-off Roach busted McConaghey's bar mirror with?"

"Are you plumb—"

"Don't ask me questions," I snarled. "Give me answers! Where is it? 'Dyou give

101

it back to 'im?"

Weak Back waggled his head. The look of his eye said he knowed I was daffy. "Course I give it back to him. It was his gun, wasn't it? I give 'im *all* his truck when I let him out like you told—"

"You seen Hack Averill's body?"

"Course. I—"

Weak Back stared and, like a card house falling, his jaw dropped open. "Jerusalem! You don't think—"

"I dunno what I think," I said; and didn't. I was that bogged down I didn't know 'jump' from 'sic 'em.' I said: "Where's Roach at now?"

"But look—" Weak Back scowled. "Roach *couldn't* of done it – killed Lou Gromm, I mean. He was locked—"

"There ain't no such word as 'couldn't'," I said. "Not when it comes to this star-packin' business. I wouldn't trust my gran'-mother even. Whoever killed Hack must've killed Lou, too—"

"Then it sure wasn't Roach. We had 'im locked in that cell. I on'y let him out just this mornin', dammit. Didn't git no chanct to, yestiday, I was too worked up about that poem of mine – an' about you gittin' run out by Curly an' his hardcases. Did they catch

102

you?"

I waved that aside. "I wouldn't be here if they had," I said. "Now look: *I* didn't kill Hack – I never had no chance to—"

"But you knew he was goin' to the Cherry-cow – Doaks told you," Weak Back said. "It's all over town. He told you Hack had got his horse and headed for Tilt's place—"

"I never got to Tilt's till noon today. Hack had already left—"

"Left!" Weak Back said. "Hell – he never even *got* there! After Roach brung in Hack's body, Jose Cuervo went out there to see, an' Tilt told him they hadn't seen Hack since the inquest."

He eyed me worried-like. "You kin tell me, boy. I'm your friend till hell freezes – an' I'll stick with you; I stick by *all* my friends. It don't make no difference t' *me* if you killed 'im – he was a damn worm anyhow an' oughta been—"

"Shut off the blat an' listen a minute. I didn't *kill* Hack; get that through your head, will you? Roach found him, didn't he? He'd been blasted wide open. Roach had a shotgun. Roach—"

"Ahr!" said Weak Back.

Which described my own notions plenty.

"Well, it damn sure wasn't *me*," I said.

103

"If it wasn't Roach, who was it?"

If Hack Averill wasn't Lou's killer, I wanted it to be Roach. I didn't like Roach, anyway – didn't cotton to nothing about him. In the first place he was a drifter; there was too many drifters in Galeyville now, guys lured by the wild tales of silver, easy pickings and high rolling. Another thing, Roach had whiskers. Not that he was the only one raised them; every third guy had a beard, far as that went. But not no beard like Mister Drifter Roach who, someway, seemed to hide behind that splash of spinach that he grew so fierce. Nor I didn't like the look of his eyes, his sneers and whinings and smart-alec talk. He was too damn smart for his britches.

What had he wanted to get put in jail for? You couldn't tell me he hadn't wanted to, else what had he busted that bar mirror for? He wasn't no damfool puncher with a load of booze tucked under his belt. There hadn't been no liquor smell on him; he had been cold sober when Weak Back grabbed him – according to Weak Back's tell of it anyhow.

"It mighta been Cuervo," Weak Back muttered, proving his thoughts hadn't been plumb idle. But his tone didn't show much enthusiasm. "Nobody's seen Jose – except me – since the inquest – me an' Tilt James, that is. An' he coulda been doing a heap o' things. Don't forget how he was snoopin' outside this winder—"

"We don't *know* he was," I argued. "We only think it was him account of them marks. We never seen him. *Anybody* might of made them heel marks. Say, for instance, they was made by his boots. What have you got? – nothing. Not a goddam thing. Even if they *was* his boots, that don't prove Jose Cuervo was in 'em! In a case like this—"

"The hell with it," growled Weak Back, blowing out his breath like he was plumb disgusted. "Listen. I got four new verses to that ballard of mine. I'd like t' git your opinion on 'em. Now—"

"Never mind that scribblin'," I said. "We got to get to the bottom of these murders. Roach busted McConaghey's mirror with a sawed-off shotgun. Ain't that what you said?"

"What of it?" grunted Weak Back grumpily.

"I don't know what of it; but I got a damn strong hunch it was a sawed-off shotgun ended Hack Averill's worries. An' Roach, don't forget, brought him in."

"But if Roach had killed Hack, bringin' in Hack's body woulda been the last thing he'd thought of," Weak Back objected.

"Mebbe not," I said. "This Roach might be smart enough to of seen we'd figure that way. When you're dealing with a killer—"

"Ol' Jawbone had t' deal with killers. He—"

"My Gawd," I said, "get your mind off that fool poetry! You got plenty to do without makin' jingles—"

"Jingles! Fer two cents—"

"I ain't got two cents. Now listen," I said, grabbing hold of his shirt sleeve, "Roach brought him in. Off the Cherrycow trail. I told Doaks I was goin' to the Cherrycow. Doaks told me Averill had gone out there. He's told half the town I went out there after him. An' Tilt James'll tell all askers *I was out there!*

"You know what I think? I think some ory-eyed son's tryin' to frame me!"

Weak Back rasped a paw crosst his cheeks – a way he has when he wants to look thoughtful. He said, kind of slow and considering, "You might be right. You was right, all right, about Hack bein' killed with a shotgun. Twenty gauge. Same gauge as Roach's gun. But that don't make Roach out the killer. An' you can't git aroun' that other part. Mister Roach was snug locked up in jail when Lou got his the other night. An' how could that drifter of killed Cramp Leyholt? He wasn't even *round* when Leyholt got killed."

"It don't have to follow that one guy rubbed the whole works out."

"It don't? How many killers you think we *got* aroun' here?"

"Well," I said, going back to my first thought, "if it wasn't Roach it must've been Joe Cuervo. He's the only hombre could of gulched them all. Unless – Say! *you* ain't gone in for killin', have you?"

"Who – *me?*" Weak Back stepped back like he saw a rattler. He wiped the sweat off his cheeks and forehead. "Don't talk like that, feller! I thought fer a secon' you *meant* it. By cripes, I don't mind admittin' there's been times in this thing when I just about thought I *must* of. I'm about the only guy in this office there ain't nobody suspicioned much. An' that's how it is in the stories, y' know; it's allus that feller what does it."

I said, "Don't talk just to hear your head rattle."

I got to thinking then about Jose Cuervo. Weak Back was right. Roach couldn't of

107

done it. Not while he was locked in the Galeyville jail.

But Cuervo'd been loose every minute of the time. Loose and unaccounted for. He *claimed* he'd been to Bandera's fiesta. But that didn't prove he had been. And what had he been doing outside that window, listening to me and Weak Back talking? He could of heard us just as good in the office. Why hadn't he wanted us to know he was listening? What had he figured to hear, I wondered. Just what the blue hell was that Mexican up to?

Another thing: Weak Back had told me just yesterday morning that Ike Shotwell, the night before – the night Lou was killed, had seen Joe Cuervo snooping round outside. According to Ike, peering into Lou's office. What for? What had he expected to see? And what *had* he seen? – the killer?

More likely, I thought, he'd been watching his chance to slip in and knife Lou.

Knifing was a Mexican's trick.

Women kind of favoured it, too.

Had it been some woman out of Lou's past that had slipped in that night and stuck my knife in him?

It could of been.

Then it come in my mind what Weak Back had told me about Hack Averill and Cuervo. About them being so late-like and secretly chummy. It was not like Averill to take up with a greaser.

Something else struck me. Like a wink of light, Cramp Leyholt's killing and the stage office stick-up had taken place on the very same night! And Leyholt's body had been found in the alley between the stage company's office and Jack Dall's place. And it had been Hack Averill, mostly, that had piled up the evidence against Cherokee Jack!

Seemed like there had ought to be something in them facts that would be worth a man's time unraveling. Seemed like I was on the right trail if I could only cut in. And I was – I admit it. I'd a part of the puzzle right under my hands.

It was then that it come to me about the paper – about the scrap of paper I had picked off the doorstep when I'd crossed to their wagon the other morning with Dora and Tilt.

I began rummaging my pockets. At last I found it. A dirty old scrap. Probably torn from a letter. There was just a handful of words on it, scrawled with a pencil:

. . . hombre you been hunting . . .
Curly Bi. . .

I stared at it frowning.

It didn't ring no bell.

It made me feel kind of foolish, special when Weak Back said, coming over and peering: "What the hell's that?"

He read it and snorted. "Where'd you get that thing?"

I told him.

He said, "You got worries more important to the state of your health than—"

He stopped abrupt-like, gone stiff and gone frozen.

I'd caught it, too.

The stealthy scrape of somebody's boot sole. Outside the window.

I thought of Joe Cuervo and reached for my pistol.

The bend of that move was the only thing saved me.

Just above my left shoulder, chunked deep in the wall, was a knife. Still quivering. It buzzed like a rattler.

I took one look and dived through the window. I fired three times at a running shape – fired again. But the light was too poor. It was too near to darkness. And the fellow was just a smidgin too fast. He got away in the shadows out back of Jack Dall's place.

I was still tearing after him when Weak Back caught me.

"By the gods!" he panted. "Ain't y' got *no* sense? Whyn't y' shout from the housetops if y' want everybody t' know that you're back here? Git goin'! Git goin'! Grab a bronc an' git goin'!"

"Leggo now – listen! I—"

"Don't be a nidjit! Don't stan' there an' argue! Grab a hawss an' *git goin!*"

Dust spurted sudden from the ground beside me. Adobe flaked from a wall by my elbow; crumbling bits rolled down off my shirtback.

The feel of it roused me. He was right. I would get no advantage out of staying here longer.

I took his advice – I took it running. Grabbed reins from a tie rack and leaped a saddle.

Chapter Ten

Jack Dall's Saloon

I TOOK his advice and I went – but not far.

I circled the camp and tore back, toward Dall's place.

We rocked into the alley.

My eyes swept its murk for some sign of that knifeman.

The back corner of Dall's was two jumps away when I kicked foot from stirrup and heaved myself off. Just a hunch, but a good one. The bronc hit the corner and went straight up with his ears back and squealing like all of hell's rusty axles squawking. He fell to the barking of somebody's gun.

I dropped flat on my belly, eyes glued to the corner.

From the street came the crowd like cow-critters stampeding.

They come fogging into the alley's mouth just as somebody – the guy, I guess, which had dropped my horse – come lamming out of the cat-black shadows.

I could see his hands cramming loads in a pistol.

I was coiling my muscles to jump and trip

him when the crowd come rushing up behind me and I didn't dare budge lest the whole pack grab me.

The running man yelled.

"I'm get hees caballo but not that Flash – she's queek lak' the wherrelwind! She must 'ave jomp; she's no back dere!"

Cuervo!

There wasn't no doubting that chopped up lingo!

So he was back, I thought, from wherever he'd been to.

He passed so close I thought sure he'd bump me.

It was a damn lucky hunch that had flattened me down there.

I hugged the wall, scarce even breathing.

"I'm teenk," Cuervo growled, "she's head for stage office—" and the whole crew whirled like a flock of sheep and went bolting back to the street again, snarling and swearing and waving their hoglegs. I could hear their wild bragging of what they would do to me.

After they'd gone I got up on my feet again. You can bet I was thankful that I still was able.

I crouched there stiffly with my eyes hunting Cuervo.

After a bit I seen him. Down there by the alley mouth. He'd not gone with the others; wasn't fixing to follow them. He had steered them off to get himself rid of them.

Why?

I watched him, determined to find out.

Flattened there against Dall's wall, I saw him flick quick looks about. Like it was *him* they'd been hunting instead of me. It sure was peculiar, the way he was acting.

With a sudden swift purpose he moved – and me after him!

He turned to the right, toward the front of Dall's bar. Was he going in? I wondered.

If he was, I would have him. Right where I wanted him.

I catfooted round, found the back door to Dall's place. And let myself in.

The place was dark. It was, also, empty. Still as the hole where we'd dumped Lou's body.

It was Dall's back room where the big games was held.

I crossed it, careful. Like a goddam spider. Found the door to the bar room and eased it open. Just a crack. Just a fraction. Just enough to see by.

And, boy, I seen plenty!

There was Cuervo, slipping through

Dall's batwings like he set considerable store on not being seen. Which proved to me that the bar room was empty. The whole camp, I guessed, had taken Cuervo's tip and rushed round to the front of the stage company's office.

Cuervo's walk was quiet as a Injun's.

His teeth was bared, and the quick, hard look he flung about held the glitter and glint of sun off a gun barrel.

Each move that he made was swiftly certain. There wasn't no groping, no wasted motion. He went to the bar, went around and behind it. Like a phantom he stooped beside Jack's iron safe.

I could hear little noises – a sudden, muffled *boom!* Smelled the damn stink as the smoke bulged around him.

By the gods, I thought, *he's robbing Jack's safe!*

It was just this way, I abruptly remembered, they had busted that twenty-five hundred cartwheels out of the safe in the stage company's office the night Cramp Leyholt had been found in the alley.

Maybe Joe Cuervo had done that, too!

Might be, I thought, this was what they'd been hatching. Him and Hack Averill with all their whisperings. The real reason back of their chancy meetings.

And then I saw further – I mean I sensed something else.

Cuervo, by grab, might of killed Cramp Leyholt. Just like I'd told Weak Back he might of! It was that alley outside where we'd found Cramp's dead carcass. Maybe Cramp had seen Cuervo slipping out of the stage office – the alley run between the stage office and Dall's. Cramp must of seen him and Cuervo had killed him to shut up Cramp's mouth!

Stranger things had happened.

In my startlement then – in my surprise and excitement, I must of pushed on the door. Anyway, it swung open. With a skreak like a gate hinge.

Cuervo jumped like a rabbit. His eyes bugged straight at me. I seen the blaze in his stare and his bared teeth glinting.

"So!" he snarled in a quick burst of breath. "I 'ave catch you tryin' for rob thees saloon!"

The sheer gall of it beat me. I gaped like a ninny. Or maybe it was the blue silk scarf adangle, smoking, in his hand that crouched me there muscle-bound and tongue-tied.

My scarf! I'd of known it anyplace! He

had used it to muffle—

He moved like chain lightning. With a lunging speed I had never suspected he hurled his crouched, wiry body sideways. His pistol swept up in a flashing arc – belched livid across the lamps' yellow gloom.

I felt the door torn out of my grasp; felt myself drove backward, stumbling, gasping.

Then I caught myself; went lunging forward. He hadn't hit me – hadn't even nicked me; both his bullets had struck the door, but the shock of them traveled my arm like the bite of a knifeblade. My gun arm, by God! – and I couldn't use it.

But there wasn't nothing wrong with my left.

I bent, grabbed my sixgun off the floor. And like that, still bent, I heard the back door suddenly open.

I was trapped. I knew it. Trapped front and rear.

I lammed myself at the big room's brightness.

A shot burst splinters from the bar beside me. A hornet's buzz zipped across my shoulder. Cuervo, back of an overturned table, was smashing wild sound against the walls with his pistol.

I drove two shots – saw the table jerk; saw the ragged hole that was punched through its surface just beside Cuervo's face.

He was firing frantic.

His hammer banged on a empty shell; and then I was past him, was shoving the batwings, was seeing their thin slats ripped and splintered by the lead droned out of that back room after me.

God knows I never expected to make it.

But make it, I did. I was suddenly through them and out on the porch, was blindly stumbling down the steps, was jerking a bronc's reins loose from the hitch rack – was into its saddle and spurring like mad.

Chapter Eleven

In The Turkey Creek Bottoms

HID away in the Turkey Creek bottoms, in a tangle of ash and sycamore, was a tiny, well-concealed shack once used as a close-to-town rendezvous by Jack Swartz and his gun-quick long riders. Jack was a

Charleston saloon keeper with an under-nourished craving for excitement. His trade never seemed quite able to busy him and he'd taken to running new brands on the side.

I knew of this hideout through Weak Back, who had ridden with Jack when he'd more ambition and less leaf lard for his horse to carry. There was a good many angles to Weak Back Jones – abilities most folks never dreamed he was up to. A case of 'still waters', I reckon. In tipping me off he had mentioned casual: "You an' me, now, is the only two jaspers in Galeyville knows this. Come you ever git into bad trouble, boy . . . go there. It's a close spot an' handy, an' Jack an' his boys ain't ridin' much these days."

I remembered another thing Weak Back had said. "One of these days we're going to find Lou croaked with a knife in his back."

And, almost on the heels of his words, that was what we *had* found.

It was damned uncanny the way his sayings come true. Nine out of ten he'd call the turn; if he'd ever gone in for gambling, I thought, he'd of cleaned out every damn hell hole in town.

But he didn't care for gambling. He

didn't seem to care about much of anything except setting around. That, and, writing fool poetry.

Just the same he was a whole heap shrewder than folks give him credit for. He was a firm believer in looking before he leaped; and he had steered me clear of trouble more than once.

It was a cold, windy night, natural weather for the Cherrycows, and lonesomer than a preacher at pay-check time when I swung through the hills on a careful-thought circle that cut Turkey Creek away east of Galeyville.

I was coming back, having firm in mind Jack Swartz's old hideout which I aimed to use if I could find any grub there. The canyon was darker than hell on holiday and I was having some trouble picking my way through the brush; I sure hadn't grabbed any shakes of a night horse. He was spooky as a rabbit. I had to keep a tight rein on him, and when I figured I must be getting well along towards the hideout I got off him and walked, being mindful to keep one hand in quick reach of his nose – he was the snortin'est critter I ever had rode on.

I could see the Galeyville lights in the distance like low-hanging stars when they

120

shone from the mesa. Case you ain't got no picture of the place I'll tell you a little more about its layout. It was started in the fall of 1880 .as a boom silver camp around John Galey's mine. It was in Turkey Creek Canyon at a place where the mountains open out like a saucer. In the center of the saucer stands a stony mesa with the town sprawled out like a drunk on the top of it. A damn good place for an owlhooter's stronghold, as Curly and his gang had seen at first glance when the Earp clan's nearness had drove them from Charleston. There was live oak and juniper growing on the mesa to afford some shade and wood for the cook fires. The taller peaks of the Cherrycows, as everybody called the Chiricahua Mountains, stand stiff to the west like the ghosts of the dead waiting round for the payoff; great towering rocks and stone-rimmed canyons, gloomy and dark as the sound of thunder. Then down in the hollow, along by the creek, was this tangle of ash and sycamore timber I'd been having such a tussle at finding my way through. From the canyon's mouth, off a whoop and a holler, you might catch a look at the San Simon Valley. Jack Swartz's old hangout wasn't much more removed from the town than a gunshot.

So much, then, for the country's layout.

I could hear the town's noises pretty damn plain, its shouts and rough laughter, its fiddling and helling. Which told me plain I must be getting close.

It must have been around ten. A lopsided bucket of a moon leered down from a rack of cloud beyond the Cherrycow rim, plating the younder mesa with silver. But it didn't reach down to the roundabout shadows that was piled deep and dark in the Turkey Creek bottoms.

I rode up on Swartz's shack with considerable caution, knowing from Weak Back's talk something of the temper of that gentleman's nerves. I rode up real slow with the twist of a tune softly wrapped round my tongue; but it looked mighty like I had the place to myself.

The corral was empty.

There was no light in the shack.

I hitched the horse to a sycamore.

"Hello . . ." I said careful. "Anybody to home?"

There didn't no one answer.

I didn't hear no one move.

So I went to the door and pulled it open.

The loudest sound I could hear was the pound of my heart.

I scratched a match on my Levis. The place was empty. I tramped on in; closed the door behind me.

I was glad to see the tow sack covering the window. I guessed I could have light without drawing no attention. I don't know why I felt any need of a light unless it was light someway made the place seem more cheerful.

There was a crazy-legged table built against one wall. A pine slat bunk built against another. A pot bellied stove held the shack's far end. On the rickety table I seen a stump of a candle in the neck of a bottle.

I lit it.

I went over to the bunk and, after looking for scorpions, sat myself down. I was tired with riding and goddam hungry. Way I felt I could of et a sidewinder, rattles and all.

Thoughts was poor fodder and they was all I had in me. If it wasn't for Dora I'd of pulled my picket pin – I was half of a mind to anyway by that time.

I say I was half of a mind to; but I wasn't, really. I knew damn well I would never go till I went on a shutter or had solved them killings. It wasn't never in us Marlatts to quit. We was a mule-minded bunch once you got our mad up.

I got to thinking about that whiskered drifter. He still seemed to me the best bet for Hack's killer; only I couldn't see why he would want to kill anyone – least of all, Hack. So far as I knew he hadn't ever met him; didn't even know, probably, Hack existed. Or hadn't, anyways, till he'd found him dead on the trail to Tilt James' place. And, like Weak Back had said, he'd been locked up in jail when Lou Gromm was killed. He'd been locked up, too, when Cramp Leyholt cashed in.

Still, as Weak Back had likewise observed, it didn't seem hardly likely there was more than one killer raising hell in our bailiwick.

Yet, when you come right down to it, why should we think that? What was Galeyville but a killers' paradise? Half the crooks in the country hung out there; renegades, horse thiefs, rustlers and what not.

On the face of the evidence though, it was Cuervo. In each case Cuervo had had the opportunity. What did we really know about Cuervo? Nothing! Not one damn thing except Lou Gromm had hired him. And what, of course, I had just discovered – that he was a fly-by-night robber. Thinking over how I'd caught him blowing Jack Dall's safe

– and with my blue scarf in his paw to leave behind for evidence, made me itch to get my hands on him. If he had robbed the safe at the stage office too, it was dollars to doughnuts he had killed Cramp Leyholt. Leyholt, drunk, had probably barged in on him. Or had seen Cuervo lugging his loot from the stage company's office.

Why, damn it, I thought, he could of killed Hack Averill. Even if they *had* been working together. He could of done it easy – could even of used Roach's sawed-off to do it with! He'd had plenty of chance to get hold of Roach's gun – plenty of chance to get it back, likewise, before Weak Back had got around to letting Roach out.

The more I thought, the more it looked like Cuervo.

If him and Hack Averill had been in this together, it would have been plain good business with him to snuff Averill. Make his grab bigger and widen his chances. The dead stay dead pretty long, as a rule; and it ain't very often you hear a dead man talk. For Cuervo to kill Hack Averill would be simply the logical result of his association with Averill.

Of course they might of fallen out over something.

But I wasn't worrying much about that part. What I couldn't figure out was why Jose Cuervo should try to pin things on me – or wasn't he? But yes; of course he was! Right from the start he'd been busy undermining me. And robbing Dall's safe with my scarf in his hand!

But *why?*

I wasn't what you'd call no Mexican hugger, but Cuervo and me had always got along all right. He minded his business and I'd minded mine. I hadn't never stepped on any of his corns that I knowed of.

It must be, I thought, he figured I was onto him.

I remembered then how he'd stood outside the office window and listened while me and Weak Back had been talking that morning. How through that same window a knife had come at me. How—

Hell, I thought; he must be getting desperate. To cover Cramp's killing he had had to kill others – Lou Gromm and Hack Averill. Or maybe Hack had killed Lou.

It didn't much matter. He must have killed Hack Averill. And he sure had built me up for the jackpot. Course it had been my own fault at the start – letting old Cherokee out like I had. I had garnered and

126

earned the whole camp's suspicion. But it looked like now Jose was getting a mite rattled. He must figure – hell, he *knew!* I had the deadwood on him; if only in the matter of Jack Dall's safe.

It was then I seen how he could fix me proper.

Joe Doaks would tell how I'd rented a horse. He'd relate I had gone to the Cherry-cow spread – that I hadn't brought the horse back. He'd done that much already.

Now he would say I had stopped by again. Hunting Hack Averill. That he'd told me Hack had gone to Tilt James' spread. Tilt would tell all concerned how I'd showed up there after he'd warned me away. Folks would think about how Roach had found Hack's body on the Cherrycow trail, and all the law west of Pecos would hunt me. Then along would come Cuervo to tell of catching me at Jack Dall's safe and the last damned nail would be slogged in my coffin.

The crunch of gravel got me off the bunk.

The door banged open and in come Dora.

Yeah. Dora James. With her taffy hair all loose and wild.

I stared. Choked a curse. Caught hold of

her wrist with my rope scarred fingers. "Shut that door," I said.

And she done it. Shut it and faced me with her eyes dark and worried-like.

I said: "How'd you guess I'd be out here?"

"Weak Back." Her voice was fogged with some urgent need. "He—"

"Never mind Weak Back! You get along out of here! What'd you reckon folks'll—"

She flung the hair back out of her eyes. Her cheeks took color and a quick breath lifted the shape of her breasts up. "Don't blame him, Flash – I *made* him tell me. I – It's that drifter, Roach! It's *him* that's been killing—"

"What!"

I expect I shook her harder than I meant to. I was near knocked out of my wits with her talking. If Roach . . .

"But he *couldn't!*" I said. "We had him locked up in the Galeyville jail!"

"I don't care! He's the one, Flash – he's the one that killed them. And Roach isn't his name – Oh, I've tried to be loyal; believe me, I have. Tried to tell myself that—"

"*Shh!*" I said; and we both of us stiffened.

Then we heard it again. The creak of

128

leather. And my horse kind of whinnied, real low and pleased like.

"There's somebody comin'. Git behind that door."

She didn't move quick enough to suit me noways. She hadn't been hunted like I had. Her nerves wasn't honed so sharp as mine. I swept her behind me. Yanked my pistol.

I seen the latch lift. Slow and real careful. Seen the door start to open – seen a crack of night through it. There wasn't no sound. Just a low, jerky breathing. That I finally decided was of my own making.

Then the snout of a gun come round the door's angle. A thick-fingered hand and the cuff of a sleeve.

I tensed. Cocked my muscles.

But too quick, with a lurch, he was into the cabin.

I found myself staring down his gun barrel.

Chapter Twelve

An Old Drunk Comes Home

HAVE I told you what Dora James looked like?

She was young. And classy as a little red wagon. She was the aim of half the men in the Cherrycows; which is the same as saying all the guys still single and otherwise able. She was easier to look at than a stick of striped candy. Slim as a willow and a heap more exciting. Rangy and quick, with her eyes always dancing and a gay little laugh always ready to tickle you. She was tall for a woman – or it might be her slimness just made you think she was; the way she carried her head, or the lift of her chin. Her eyes was different, too. Like violets. Just now, in the candle flame, they looked dark. And big. And kind of scared, I thought; which was odd, because everyone knew she wasn't scared of nothing.

Course it might of been just the way Weak Back had come in on us. So kind of sudden and stealthy like.

I seen him stare and blink.

Then a sheepish grin broke the set of his features. And he lowered his gun and kind of colored a little. "Well . . ." he said. "I couldn't be sure . . ."

He put away his gun.

I didn't sheath mine.

"Thought mebbe," I told him, "you come t' collect the reward on me, Weak Back."

He snorted. Then said with his eyes all squinched up: "They've sure got one *on* you! 'F you'd took my advice an' sloped like I tol' you, you'd never got in such a Gawd-awful mess. You allus *was* such a mule fer— Can't *you* talk him round t' clearin' out awhile, Dora?"

I said: "I aim to get my hands on that killer first. I'll get him, too—"

"Not as no lawman you won't. The city fathers has done come round an' took your badge an' 'thority away fr'm you. Joe Cuervo's marshal of Galeyville now. Seems t' set real store on gettin' shut of you. Got a reward put on you – 'Dead or Alive' is the way he's made it; an' it don't make no difference how the bullet gits you. There's posses a-scourin' all through these hills fer you. An' it ain't fer them killin's. It's fer bustin' open the strongbox in Jack Dall's saloon."

Weak Back scrubbed his knuckles on the

legs of his Levis. "You sure are gettin' up in the world. Just a couple more jerks an' they'll dangle you permanent."

I remembered Dora.

She was eyeing me like they'd dabbed their rope over the limb already.

I said, "You got to get outa here, Dora."

"Never mind about me—"

"You heard what Weak Back said. 'Dead or Alive.' There'll be a heap of shootin' when that bunch sights me—"

"They won't *dare* shoot if they see me with you—"

"For five hundred dollars," Weak Back said; and thought better of it. "Where's your father at, Dora?" he asked.

"In town. Isn't he? He was there when—"

"Taken a room at the hotel, has he?"

She nodded, eyes questioning.

I stared at Weak Back some on my own hook.

He said, "What did you want to see Flash about, Dora?"

I told him. "She's got some wild idea Ed Roach is the killer—"

"He *is!*" she cried. "I'm sure he is—"

"Because of that letter your father wrote him?"

132

"Not because of—" That was where she stopped. Right sudden.

I seen the change that come over her face; saw the sharp, quick look she flung at Weak Back. Saw Weak Back grin.

I didn't cotton to it.

"You're wonderin'," he said, "how I know he wrote him. Matter of fact, ma'am, I saw the letter – bulk of it, anyhow. Our friend Flash has the rest. He picked it up off the doorstep the other day. I expect Roach figured he was pretty dang cute, tearin' it up that way before we could search him. But I seen him drop it. I never let on when I locked him up; but afterwards I come back an' hunted.

"I've pieced it together. What I found, I mean. Want to see it?"

All I could do was stand and stare at him. Remember what I said? – about there being more to him than a fellow would think for?

"Yes," Dora's voice was almost a whisper. "Yes . . . I do. Where is it?"

Weak Back stood a mite. Thoughtful. Like he was considering whether as an officer of the law, he had better show it to her or not. At last he shrugged. Thrust a hand in the pocket of his lemon colored shirt and brought forth from its depths several wrinkled scraps of dirty paper.

"I reckon you got a right to know what your ol' man's been up to," he grumbled. "Come over here to the light and we'll fit the piece Flash got into the rest of it."

Digging the 'Curly Bil' scrap from one of my own pockets I followed Weak Back and Dora over to the table. I gave Weak Back my piece and we watched him arrange them. We had the most of it.

Here's the way the thing looked when he finished:

> Dear D
> It will be to your advantage to take in the sights of Galeyville. That hombre you been hunting is here.
> Curly Bil.

"But that can't be it," Dora said, looking relieved. "My father's name isn't – Why, it's signed 'Curly Bill'."

"Yeah," Weak Back said. "But your father wrote it."

Catching the look of our eyes Weak Back grunted. "Mister Tilt James wrote it," he repeated, grim like. "Look it over, ma'am –

134

you know his writin' better'n I do. Notice that *B*. Either of you ever know anybody else t' make a *B* like that?"

When nobody answered, Weak Back sniffed. "Course you don't. Nobody but Tilt ever made 'em like that. I'm a handwritin' expert – ef I *do* say it as shouldn't. I've spent a mort o' time off 'n' on studyin' out the funny things a fella will do when he gits a pencil into his mit. It's Tilt's writin', all right. I'll swear to it on a stack of Bibles higher'n the smokestack on Galey's smelter."

His satisfaction kind of got in my hair. I said, "You saw that drifter tear this up, you say? Saw him yourself, did you? An' you're sure this here is what you *saw* him tear up?"

"Said so, didn't I? Then what're you tryin' t' do? Make me out a liar, or somethin'?"

"It's a serious thing," I told him darkly, "to accuse a man—"

"He shoulda thought of that 'fore he wrote it," scowled Weak Back. " 'Fore he sharpened the point on his dad-rammed pencil."

I looked at Dora.

Dora nodded. "I guess he's right. It looks like Dad's writing."

There was a pinched kind of look got about her mouth and a downhill drag to the points of her shoulders that made me feel like choking Weak Back. But that's the way he was put together. He could no more see he was hurting Dora than he could of cut a slice of green cheese from the moon. When the jaws of his mind got a hold on a thing he worried it like a dog would a bone.

"Notice the tail of that *y*," he pointed. "Your ol' man allus flings his *y*'s aroun' that way. An' that *I* an' them *g*'s – Hell! We won't hev no trouble provin' Tilt wrote it."

I gnashed my teeth and looked away from Dora. "All right; drop it," I said. And then, to Dora: "This Roach the 'friend' your dad's been expectin'?"

She didn't have to answer. I could see he was by the look of her.

Some unwelcome thoughts got afoot in my mind. I said, "What makes you think so?"

I seen her kind of wince. Then she pulled her chin up and faced me squarely.

"Because Dad said the other night that his friend had got here, and was 'big a fool as ever.' That he'd 'gone and busted' McConaghey's bar mirror and gotten himself 'clapped in jail first pop'."

"You see?" Weak Back grinned. "I told you so. However," he added with a grin at Dora, "it don't make no difference. Don't none of it make no never-mind noways. Tilt's friend never killed Lou Gromm – never had no chanct to, even if Lou was the guy he was huntin'. Which we don't know he was, an' he prob'ly wasn't. Roach was still locked up a considerable while after we found Lou dead. He was still locked up. You can't git around it."

"And," I said, from a pile of wondering, "he hadn't hit town when Cramp Leyholt was killed. So he couldn't of blown Cramp's light out, neither."

After that talk kind of petered out. We stood around looking glum for a spell; me raking my head for something to say that might cheer up Dora, who looked like the whole thing was someway her fault – which, of course, it wasn't. It was mine. I reckoned, as much as anyone's because maybe if I hadn't let Cherokee Jack loose there might none of these killings ever got started.

It just went to show, I thought, kind of bitter like, what comes of a fellow trying to mix his oar into someone else's business.

I said, to be talking, "How's your poem

137

comin', Weak Back?"

I thought that would perk him up some, but it didn't. He scowled and spat. "Fer two cents," he said, flexing up his fingers, "I'd make that dadburned drummer eat it!"

"Drummer?"

"Yeah. I showed it to that cawfee drummer that come in on the stage this afternoon. That fella ain't got no more idea of poetry than a damn ol' sow's got of cleanin' a six-gun. Showed 'im the best durn verse I had, too – the new ones; them four I wrote after Roach come in packin' Hack Averill's mortal remains on his saddle. Hell!"

"Don't believe I've heard them, have I?"

"*You* wouldn't keer fer 'em."

"Mebbe," I said, "Miz' Dora would."

He kind of chirked up a little at that and made a great show of hunting his clothes for them, finally getting them out of his wallet. "It's about a fella called Jawbone the Loose-Mouth," he told her. "I'm goin' t' leave it right up t' you, ma'am, if these here verses ain't consid'able better'n the gosh-awful slush that Roman wrote—"

"Roman?" I said, surprised in spite of myself. I hadn't heard there was any Romans in town. I'd supposed they was all dead long ago. "What Roman?" I said.

138

"Why, that Shakespear fella," Weak Back growled at me, like he was disgusted anyone should be so ignorant.

"Oh!" I said, and closed my mouth up. Didn't seem to be no use in me telling him Shakespear was a Portuguese. If Weak Back wanted to make him out a Roman I didn't guess nobody would kick much. "You don't want to pay no notice to drummers," I told him. "They ain't got no savvy. If they had they wouldn't be drummers. Go ahead an' read it."

"Well . . . if you insist:

"A schemin' connivin' obstreperous rascal,
    Joe Choler got hep to Jawbone's hidden mine—
Swore by his tintype that cache he would locate;
    An' when he had done so Jawbone should assign.

"Joe gathered his gang an' he gave 'em instructions,
    A long-winded talk about bumpin' gents off—
This slick jasper Jawbone's death had t' be certain;

139

As certain as hellfire before they could scoff.

"They trailed him by inches with Indian trackers,
They tracked him crost desert an' mountain an' stream—
They trailed him by day an' by night, week an' fortnight;
But all that they got was a chance to blaspheme.

"It wore down their patience an' frazzled their tempers,
An' learned them new cuss words t' use by the score—
It got them much sunburn an' sandburn an' blisters;
An' anger an' heart ache – but no sign of ore.

"There she is," he said. "What do you think of her? Ain't that better'n Shakespear's stuff? Hell! They's sense to this! Where's the sense sayin' a rose would smell the same by some other name? I'll leave it up t' *any*one if that ain't the damnedest—"
He broke off so sudden-like I looked up from my brooding. I seen the queerest look

on Weak Back's face. He was standing there with the paper still in his hand, staring at nothing like he was seeing something.

"Great guns!" he muttered, hoarse like. "I plumb forgot what I come out here for! Jerusalem! I come out here t' tell you Cherokee Jack's back!"

"Back!" I snarled; and then I seen it. I swore an oath and jumped for the door.

But Weak Back grabbed me as I was yanking it open.

"Here! Where you off to?" And "*Flash!*" Dora cried.

Her eyes was like two holes in a blanket.

But I couldn't help it. I'd recollected something – knew what a fool I'd been. I was remembering plenty things now I'd ought to of thought of sooner. Things left unsaid. Things small and obscure as the flick of an eyebrow.

I remembered, among other things, telling Lou that night that we'd ought to be letting that drifter, Roach, out. I remembered Tilt's threats and the things they sprang from. I recalled of a sudden the look of the office when I'd gone in with Cuervo and we'd found Lou dead with the haft of my knife sticking out from his shoulders – a pity I'd not thought of that before! There had been no signs of frenzy round him; no least sign of violence but the blood . . . the blood, and the blade of my Bowie driven deep in his gullet.

I should of seen it right off. Should of guessed at once the truth of this business. I'd had all of the pieces but no sense to arrange them.

But that was past. From here on out things was going to be different.

"Where you off to?" Weak Back growled again.

I shoved him loose.

"I'm goin'," I said, "to arrest Lou's killer!"

Chapter Thirteen

"It Mighta Been You!"

THERE's times, I guess, in every gent's life when he feels like taking a dose of mule medicine, or something. When Weak Back told us Cherokee was back, it come over me what a damned fool I'd been. It wasn't that Cherokee's coming back had anything to do with it. The surprise just kicked my wits into working.

It was the lack of havoc we had found in Lou's office – remembrance of it, I mean – that started the thoughts turning round in my mind. It was then I seen the pattern of the thing. Crimes fall in patterns. Just like all the ways of a man's life makes a pattern. He may do a few things that ain't got no place in it, but you can trace that back to the Adam in him; the desire to be different, to commend him to notice.

Like Weak Back's versifying.

Cherokee Jack, like I've said, was just a plain old soak. A drunk old has-been what, most of the time, didn't even know enough to wipe his mouth off proper. You'll reckon I expect, that wouldn't keep him from killing Lou Gromm and them other fellows. And you'd be right, thinking that. There's been plenty folks killed by half wits and nitwits. But I'll show you how I knew right then old Cherokee Jack couldn't of killed the marshal.

Cherokee had always had a violent temper. That, and his love for rotgut, was the most outstanding things about him. I expect, in his time, that temper had made him dangerous. It might have been temper,

143

away back, that had turned him to riding the owlhoot trails. But since I'd known him it had only made him look foolish; like his crying and raving when Cramp Leyholt that night had pitched him out in the street. Anger, to be dangerous and effective, has got to have some way of satisfying itself. Anger, with Cherokee, had took a childish streak. He was so full of booze, most times, he couldn't even steer himself. So, just like a kid, when something riled him more than usual, he'd look around for something to bust. I had seen him in action six or eight times. They was all of a pattern; he'd grab up whatever was handy and go to busting up everything in reach, till his strength give out or somebody stopped him. I had seen him, one night, clean out the bar of the Pioneer House – which was over in Shakespeare – just because the apron give out he wouldn't sell him no more. Cherokee busted every bottle they had in the place.

But there wasn't nothing busted in Lou Gromm's office.

Not even so much as the edge of one paper.

The place looked same as it always had, except for Lou dead with his face on the desk and my big Bowie sticking out of his shoulders. Near as I could learn, it had been the same with Hack Averill. Had Cherokee killed him, it seemed to me there'd of been more than one hole shot through Hack's body. Cherokee's rage wouldn't of quit at one. Then too, I couldn't think of no reason for Cherokee *wanting* to kill Hack. Had you asked me to bet, I'd of said they hadn't likely exchanged more than ten words in their lives. They wasn't even nodding acquaintances.

Cramp Leyholt's killing was something else.

Cramp, I was convinced, had been killed by Cuervo coming out of the stage company's office with that $2,500 from the stage company's safe. There wasn't, as I saw it, any rage in the business. Cuervo, no doubt abetted by Hack, had been lugging that loot off when Leyholt, like as not pretty well weighted with a load of Dall's coffin varnish, come staggering down that alley and seen him. Cuervo probably seen right off it was either kill Cramp or half the loot with him. He probably shot the second he seen Cramp coming.

Cuervo *could* have killed Hack.

He could have killed him for any number of reasons.

Hack hadn't never been known for his charity. He had a damn sharp tongue, and he didn't like Mexicans. He was the grasping kind who'd be sure to want more than his share of the loot. He was a blackleg lawyer from Fort Huachuca, used to the shifts and dodges of the law; a man who could pretty well be counted on to hog all the profits and shift all the blame. A slick talking article with nothing to tie to.

When Weak Back told me of Cherokee's return I didn't do no lingering to think of these things. They was in my mind without no thinking. The thought I had that had shoved me doorwards was about that drunk old Cherokee Jack.

But I wasn't first out of that cabin by no means.

Dora went past me like I was standing still. Was into her saddle before I could catch her.

I screeched, I reckon, about as loud as hell's hinges. But it wasn't no manner of use. Not noways. She never even paused; never slowed nor nothing. She was into her saddle and off like a shot.

If I'd stopped to think it would have got me wondering.

But I didn't.

Riding through her dust I was mad as a hatter. And scared, too, kind of. No telling what she'd run into – or who.

I put that bronc up the trail to the mesa like the grade wasn't no more than going up a ant hill. I never give no notice to Weak Back's mutterings; I don't guess I realized he was even within miles of me. My mad was peeling off a little, and I'd got to probing somewhat into the whats and whys of this bloody business. But I heard the shot just as plain as Weak Back.

We didn't pick no daisies, but there was a crowd building fast in the street when we got there. Fellows come rushing from every whichway, adding to the bunch already gathered. Across their shoulders, in the light of their lanterns, we could see the dark blotch in the road's yellow dust; and by McConaghey's flares I could see Pat O'Day, one of Curly Bill's hands, standing over it. He had a long-tom cuddled in the crook of an elbow. A stringer of smoke was licking up from its barrel.

Keeping hold of the reins I jumped out of the saddle. Without asking no man's pardon – never once thinking of the risk I was running – I shoved through the crowd and come up to O'Day. He was a big hulking

Mick. There was blood on his shirtfront.

The blotch in the roadway was Cherokee Jack.

Then O'Day looked up and his eyes was glinting as he give me a grin across the barrel of his rifle. He never give back an inch. Just stood there waiting. Just stood there, watchful, rubbing one hand on the slack of his Levis.

"You featherbrained fool!" I growled. "Did you kill him?"

"An' who're you t' be callin' the likes of me names? Mister Marshal-Killer Marlatt! Hoity-toity! Did ye kill 'im, he says!"

I shoved past his rifle and reached for his shirtfront.

"I asked you a question an' I'll have a decent answer—"

"Ahr – you an' yer answers!"

He backed off, scowling, with his beady eyes slitted. I seen him swap his hold to the barrel of his rifle like he'd use it for a club and maybe beat my brains out.

I said: "There's been enough trouble round here—" and someone yowls, "That's what *we* think! You keep your hands off Pat or—"

I never paid no attention. I said, "Put that gun up, O'Day, and answer me. Did

148

you kill him or didn't you?"

"If you'd clean out your ears you wouldn't hev t' ask questions!"

It was then I realized old Jack was still breathing.

The sound was like a faroff engine's moan. A kind of rasping wheeze that would make your flesh creep.

I bent down, softly cursing, beside him.

His eyes come open as I raised his head. There wasn't no recognition in them – wasn't nothing but wildness.

"Roa—" he mumbled; and his head rolled loose like. His face went twisted like a fit had grabbed it and the clutch of his hand on my arm jerked tighter.

But his jaws seemed locked. He couldn't open them. His staring eyes glazed and he gasped and was gone.

I lowered Jack's head to the ground and got up.

O'Day and me exchanged thoughtful glances.

Like he hated to do it, he finally nodded. "I seen the murtherin' blatherskite," he said – "took a crack at 'im with me rifle, b'gorra. But the devil was too fast fer me."

I had seen, quick as I stooped there beside him, that Cherokee hadn't been

149

killed by no gunshot. There was a six-inch gash slashed across his chest that anyone short of a downright fool could of told right off only a knife could of made.

So I accepted Pat's story.

I swore, impatient. Seemed like I was a fool for luck – the kind of luck nobody else wanted.

I said, "If you seen him, looks like you oughta have some notion who he was," and O'Day kind of smiled.

It was then I noticed the looks of the rest of them. They was all around me; and something in my mind turned over sudden. Something in my stomach turned over, too.

O'Day said, real soft:

"It mighta been *you*."

Chapter Fourteen

In Again, Out Again

IT was then that I remembered the reward Cuervo had posted. 'Dead or Alive' he'd made it – and I guessed, by the looks, he had made it real tempting. There wasn't

150

much needed to start this crowd acting. You could see mighty plain who they figured was the killer.

"We've still got some law in this camp," O'Day muttered. "The cartridge-case kind. Put your han's up, Marlatt."

I said: "That's pretty loud talk to be handin' a lawman—"

A sour kind of smile crossed O'Day's freckled face. "To be handin' a lawman – yeah," he said. "But you ain't no lawman; not no more, you ain't. You chucked in your star when you busted Dall's safe. Git your han's up, now, an' don't give me no back talk."

"I don't suppose you'd care to know the truth of that—"

"For Christ's sake," somebody said. "You gonna let 'im argue you out of it? Shoot the bastard an' git it done with!"

"Now look, boys—"

"We've looked long enough – an' listened, too. Shuck outa that gun belt an' put up your hands," snarled a red-shirted miner, "before I play you a tune on my six-shooter!"

"Hold on, you fellas!"

That was Weak Back's voice, and I was sure glad to hear it.

He come plowing through the crowd, never minding the growls they loosed, and spraddled his thick legs wide beside me. He said, "This tomfoolery has gone far enough! Just because Lou was killed with Marlatt's knife ain't no reason fer figgerin' Marlatt done it – no more reason than fer thinkin' he killed Hack Averill just because Roach found Hack on the Cherrycow trail an' a halfwit like Doaks tells you Flash was out there. Jerusalem! *Any*body coulda been on that trail – why pick on Marlatt? It ain't like if him an' Hack had had any reason t' kill off each other. Only thing between them two was both of 'em wanted t' court Miz' Dora. Criminy! Would one fella shoot another jest account of they—"

"Goddam right he would!" Jim Hughes shouted. And Doaks said: "If y' could of seen his *eyes*—"

"Eyes!" snorted Weak Back. "What's eyes got t' do with it? I guess you'll be tryin' t' tell me next he killed Lou Gromm account of that fuss they had! All Flash claimed was Lou was tryin' t' frame ol' Cherokee—"

"All right, Weak Back," I said, trying to shut him off. I knew he was doing his best to help me, but it looked like my chances would be better without it. The flares, playing over them roundabout faces, showed their scowls to be getting more uglier and uglier.

"We'ell . . ." said Weak Back, and paused, undecided. Then, like he had just remembered it, he said defiant-like: "As fer Cramp Leyholt—"

"Yeah. What about Cramp?" somebody grumbled.

"Well, nothin' much; only you oughtn't pay too much notice t' Cramp orderin' Flash t' keep plumb away from him – lots of guys gits sore with a fella when they owe 'im money they do' wanta pay back. Same with ol' Tilt. He was mad, is why he ordered Flash off the Cherrycow. But Flash never killed *him*, did he? 'Course not! I know things looks mighty bad fer 'im, but—"

I kind of lost track of the talk after that.

I seen I had cut my string too short. Weak Back was doing the best he knew how, but I'd of been better off if he hadn't done nothing.

I could tell them the truth, but who would believe it?

It was then I looked up and seen Curly Bill coming. Three-four of his cronies was coming right back of him.

All I'd get, waiting, was a harp and a halo.

I grabbed for Pat's rifle – got a hold on its barrel. I jammed the butt hard against Pat's fat belly. He doubled up sudden with the breath whooshing out of him. I swung with the rifle for a guy reaching hipward. The rifle butt took him on the side of the head.

Curly Bill's beller must of reached clear of Charleston.

Three-four guns started barking. Their lead sang a chorus. The crowd didn't wait around for no encore. They scuttled like ants from a burning log.

Me, too!

I went through McConaghey's bar like a cyclone.

Somebody must have heaved a bottle at me. It hit the door as I slammed it behind me.

It was darker than hell's pocket in the alley behind the place. I flattened myself against the wall by the door. It banged open sudden, hiding me proper, as five-six fellows rushed out in the alley, waving their six-shooters and swearing like mule-skinners.

"Which way you reckon he went?" cried Hughes, hoarse like.

"Prob'ly lit out fer them live oaks back

there—"

"C'mon, then – let's git 'im!"

"Hold on!" Doaks screaked. "He's got Pat's rifle—"

They lit out anyway, stumbling over the bottles and cans and making more noise than hell on a platform.

I didn't lose no time.

I ducked around the door and into McConaghey's.

Like I'd figured, it was empty.

So was the street – except for Jack's body, and the gent I had hit on the side of the head. He was coming around and groaning plenty. But the rest was all gone rushing round in the darkness, taking shots at each other and raising hell general.

I looked at the horses tied to the hitch rail.

I picked me out a long-legged black; snatched loose his reins and jumped for the saddle. I was just settling into it when a window banged up in the hotel yonder and Tilt James howled: "Git outa that saddle!"

We left town like a rocket with James' lead for the stick.

Chapter Fifteen

The Shape In The Shadows

EVER since I'd known of him, Tilt James had had the name of being 'unreliable as a woman's watch'.

A lot of folks held him just plain ornery and they weren't more than two-thirds wrong in it. But it was stubbornness got him most of his cussing – stubbornness and a plain mare's bitch of a temper. Once he got his mind made up to something, all hell couldn't swerve him. He might be more wrong than two left legs – and more like than not, he'd know it; but he'd no more consider changing his stand than a lunger could heave a bull by the tail. Get the old coot mad and you'd a war on your hands, and there was no holds barred in the Cherry-cow's warfare.

I knew all this from having worked for him. And that wasn't all I knew by a jugful. He'd squeeze a penny till the feathers fell out of the Injun's bonnet – but he had his more generous moments, too – like the time he sunk money into a paper for Galeyville. Had a printing press lugged out clear from the east, and a shanty put up for the fellow to print it in, but there never was more than three issues. One of Curly Bill's tough bucks hitched his horse to the shanty's ridgepole (account of the paper telling the truth about Curly), then fired off his pistol alongside its ear. When the dust cleared away there wasn't enough left of that printing plant to wad a twenty gauge shotgun with. Old Tilt was mad enough to eat a skunk with the hair on and swore to get even if it was the last thing he did. He *got* even, too, but that ain't got nothing to do with this story.

You'd of thought, though, with me having worked for him – and having a eye on his daughter and all, he'd of made some exceptions in his war on Galeyville. But that wasn't old Tilt's way. With him things was either black or white, one. He went whole hog when his mad was got up – I had ought to of recollected it sooner.

But late is a whole heap better than never. I was giving it thought right now – aplenty.

I was giving that letter he'd written some thought, too; and his trick signing Curly Bill's name to it.

I could see now where it come into this business; and who, by grab, he had written it to. I could see a whole heap of things now, all right. I had got my eyes plumb open and could name the killer just as easy as swearing – I expect you can, if you've read this far. There was just one fellow it *could* be; and I aimed to get my paws on him pronto!

I quit town like a twister. But I didn't go far. Just far enough to get me into the darkness and out of their sight. Then, still going hellity larrup, I tied the reins snug to the saddle horn and jumped from the bronc in them trees by the smelter. I left O'Day's long-tom rifle there and scurried back up the mesa by a cow path I knew of that would take me out back of Shotwell's store.

It did.

I snuck to a corner facing the street just in time to see the last of a big batch of riders go tearing down into the Turkey Creek bottoms, firing and shouting like a bunch of damn Injuns.

"Let 'em shout," I muttered, and shook my fist at them. I knew what I had to do now, by grab, and their going wouldn't hamper me none whatever.

Keeping well back in the shadows I worked around back of Jim Johnson's old shack where I could get a look at Doaks' corral, at the same time keeping my eyes on the hotel. When Tilt made ready to go for his horse, I aimed to know it and get there before him.

And I'd of done it, too, if it hadn't been for John Ringo.

John was Curly Bill's right bower, a slick gun artist and the most reckless damn ranny that ever struck Galeyville. A tall buck, saturnine, quick and lean. Somewhere in his past he'd got a good education and never used nothing less than fifty cent words. Just the same he was a fellow to tie to; when he give you his word he kept it.

He give *me* the word just as I started on a trot for Doaks' stable.

I'd been watching the place for a long ten minutes – the hotel, too; and not a dang sign of Tilt James had I seen. It didn't look natural for him to wait so long. Been a heap more in keeping for him to of gone right off. Right after he missed me when he fired from the window.

It had got in my mind maybe that's what he *had* done.

Determined to find out, and half scared that he had, I was starting out of the deep gloomed shadows when Ringo's voice said soft at my elbow: "Just keep ahold of your breath for a second and don't do nothing I

159

wouldn't do, Marlatt."

You could of knocked me over with no more than a whistle.

I knew it was Ringo – you couldn't mistake Ringo's soft, cultured accents. Nor there wasn't no mistaking what he'd shoved in my side.

It was the action end of a .44 Colt.

"Now, look, John," I said, "I'm damn well in a hurry. I know Curly Bill don't like me none an' has give out his orders concernin' me – but this here's *important*."

Ringo wasn't impressed.

"Importance," he said, "is always relative, Marlatt. Ever study the theory of relativity? Very interesting. Matter of reciprocal dependence, so to speak. One thing hinging on another. There is even a school of philosophy that believes implicitly—"

"I don't care what it believes! Unless I'm away off in my figurin', there's murder afoot in that stable yonder—"

"Murder? Hmm. You should learn to employ a more restrained vocabulary. What is murder but a state of—"

"Murder," I growled, "is a dead man, dammit! Unless you're wantin' to get yourself included you better stow that mouth wash an' gimme a hand here. Tilt

160

James—"

"Ah . . . James, eh?" Ringo chuckled in that soft, dry way he had. "A very complex gentleman. Also brash, but fairly truthful – so long as it suits his book, that is. You should never—"

"Never," I said, "is a damn long time, an' I've wasted all the time I aim to! Shoot if you got to; but, unless you do, I'm a'goin' to that stable an'—"

"Right," Ringo said. "Once you start a thing, go through with it regardless. Just like I told Curly Bill this evening; if we had more lawmen with your ability—"

"You'd have the whole Territory stripped by this time! Never mind the compliments," I told him bitterly. "I know I'm a jughead without you're tellin' me, but if you want to see Lou's killer caught—"

"Then you're of the opinion there is just one skunk behind all these killings?"

I said, "I ain't got no time to go into that now, but—"

"You know, I suppose, that when Weak Back told you he let Roach out this morning he was lying, don't you?"

I guess my mouth fell open. I probably swore. But it wasn't his calling Weak Back a liar that knocked the wind plumb out of me.

It was his being hep to what Weak Back had told me. I had guessed quite a while ago Weak Back was lying when he claimed he had loosed Brother Roach this morning. Weak Back had done a heap of things besides steal cattle with old Jack Swartz.

Ringo chuckled in the gloom beside me. "I use my ears when the occasion offers. I reckoned you would see through it, give you time enough."

"If you've fit Weak Back into these crazy killin's, what's your outfit so hellbent on gettin' my scalp for?"

"Well," Ringo sighed, "like maybe you've noticed, Curly Bill's a mite stubborn. He'll come round in time." He shrugged. Put his gun up. "So you think our man's in Doaks' stable, do you?"

But I wasn't stopping for no more chin music. Minute he put up his gun, I started.

He was right on my heels when we both stopped sudden.

Off yonder was tumult; a swift blur of movement. The earth threw wild sound from an oncoming pony. A rider's black shape burst out of the shadows. I heard Ringo swear. Then I seen who it was and cold fear clawed through me.

162

It was Dora James with her yellow hair flying.

Chapter Sixteen

Doaks' Stable

"DORA! Stop!" I hollered; and seen her look around wild like.

Then she saw who it was, or maybe savvied my voice. Her horse brought up, skidding, in a cloud of white dust.

"Flash!" she gasped, and looked for a moment like she'd fall from the saddle. "Quick!" she cried. "Doaks' stable – *hurry!*"

She whirled her horse and we sprinted after her.

It sort of seemed like we wasn't the only ones. The wind harried shadows was filled with movement, deceptive and spooky with the moon playing over them; but both me and Ringo was a heap too busy to give any heed to what others was up to. Leastways, *I* was. Ringo's long legs was some hard to keep up with. Then I seen him reach down

– yank his white handled sixguns.

Now that what I was afraid of had probably happened, there was a lot of things plaguing my mind – bringing sweat out. I was remembering things that fit in with my theory. All that batch of forgotten trifles that loom so big at a puzzle's solving. The disjointed phrases and half-forgot other things that had been at the back of my mind all this while. For nearly an hour now I had known who the Galeyville killer must be – who had driven my knife into Lou's bent body – who had gunned Hack Averill on the Cherrycow trail and done all the rest of them gut-shriveling didos. The look of the office should of told me right off that Lou's had been a careful-planned killing – the thing touching off this whole hellbent chain. It wasn't no spur-of-the-moment – no slash-and-stab business. No messy job, like Hack's, with a shotgun.

Lou's death was the start – I was sure of that now. Cramp Leyholt's killing was something else, connected, of course, but not in the scheme of things – nothing to do with the murderer's intention. His only aim had been to kill Lou Gromm – the rest was done to cover his part in it, to act as red herrings and throw the blame elsewhere.

164

That I got most of it, I guess, was my own fault; I had opened the ante by loosing old Cherokee. The killer was slick – had made use of my foolishness. But all he'd been after, to begin with, was Lou; the rest was defensive, things done to protect him, to keep his neck from the hangman's rope.

But he wasn't going to do it – not if *I* could help it!

I was all through with sentiment, and sympathy, too. I had learned my lesson with Cherokee Jack.

A lantern spread light just inside the barn's entrance.

I looked straight into Tilt James' black eyes.

"God, Flash!" he muttered.

The pitch of his voice held a new, queer quaver.

"Lookit there! Lookit that!"

Another sprawled shape . . . Another red stain.

It was Cuervo Tilt's shaking hand was pointing at.

He was over there, yonder, by the back of the stable. With his body half shoved out of sight in a feed rack. All you could hear was the drip of his blood as it fell off the knife hilt and pooled on the planking.

Then I heard a vast sigh and I seen the crowd round us. There was an ugly feel to the look of their faces. I seen Roach, the drifter, and Pat O'Day, John Galey and Dawson – McConaghey, too. And over by the door, blocking escape behind us, was Shotwell and Haddon, with a bunch of Curly Bill's outfit looking over their shoulders.

Tilt James' eyes was bright and watchful. He stood with his burly shoulders crouched like.

Dora's cheeks was haggard. They looked as white as a wagon sheet.

Her eyes was pleading. She said: "Flash don't—"

"Gents," I broke in, "there's a pile of you here that figures I'm the one that's been doin' these killin's. But I ain't. When I kill somebody you'll know it, by grab – I won't go round tryin' to duck what comes after. I don't mind admittin' I let Cherokee Jack loose – he never killed Cramp; Lou was set to frame him.

"So I let him skip – but I didn't kill Lou, nor any the rest of 'em."

Curly Bill come shoving his bold way forward, brushing Ike Shotwell out of his path. I seen his jaw open.

I said, "Let me finish. The coroner's jury, under advice from Lou, laid Cramp's killin' onto Cherokee Jack. Lou had his reasons for workin' things that way; but it was Jose Cuervo that killed Cramp Leyholt. Cuervo and Hack Averill had cooked up a plan to loot this here town – Cuervo to do the work, Hack to clear him if Cuervo got caught. It's my guess Lou was in on it, but it don't noways matter.

"Cuervo slipped on the first job he tackled. He come lugging a coin sack out of the stage office an' run smack into Cramp Leyholt – and gunned him. It was the only way he could shut Cramp's mouth. I think mebbe Cherokee seen that killin'. Anyway, Lou jailed him. Aimed to see that he swung. Cherokee, naturally, was scared plumb stiff: that's howcome him to run off at the head like he done."

I was taking a breath to give them the rest of it, when Curly Bill, sneering, asked, "What the hell's that got to—"

"Do with Lou's killin'?" I said. "I'll be comin' to that if you'll just keep your shirt on. Most of these hombres was someway mixed up in it. Cuervo, Hack Averill and Lou – also Weak Back and Tilt. Somehow

167

Hack stumbled onto who Lou's killer was. He tried to cash that knowledge and got cashed in instead.

"Cuervo must of known I had loosed old Cherokee. He got scared mebbe Cherokee had blabbed to me and that I'd spill the beans about him robbin' the stage office. Yesterday mornin', while Weak Back an' me was talkin' things over, Cuervo was outside the window tryin' to get him an earful. We found his tracks. The killer was listening in on our talk, too – heard Weak Back tell me Ike Shotwell seen Cuervo sneakin' round outside about the time Lou got that knife in his gizzard."

I jerked a thumb at Joe Cuervo's body. "Right there, gents, is the killer's answer. He seen how Hack had got wise to his business. Like in the case of Hack, he wasn't takin' no chances. Killin' is like that – kill one fella an' you got to kill others to keep folks from findin' out you killed the first guy."

"All right," Curly Bill growled. "We've heard enough o' your chin music, Marlatt. Get down t' cases. If you ain't the one that killed Lou, who *did* kill him?"

"Tilt James killed him," John Ringo drawled.

"No he didn't," I cut in pronto, quick lest Tilt should grab out his sixgun. "Tilt—"

"I say Tilt killed him," Ringo purred, real soft like. "Weak Back showed me the letter Tilt—"

"Tilt wrote a letter, but you never saw it. That epistle Mister Weak Back's been showin' around was written by Weak Back," I said and meant it. "Incidental like, Curly, he signed your name to it – he meant folks to *think* Tilt James had wrote it. Done a clever job, too – even fooled Miz' Dora. But he made one slip: The letter said: *'Dear D— It will be to your advantage to take in the sights of Galeyville. That hombre you been hunting is here.'* Tilt James never used the word 'advantage' in his life – not as *I* ever heard of, anyway. Weak Back was always usin' it – always bringin' it in like he brought in his brother. If I had one guess I'd say straight off that Mister Weak Back, right this minute, is raisin' a dust towards the Mexican Border."

Curly Bill let out a roar. "So it was that mealy-mouthed, jingle-brained Weak Back, was it? By cripes, I'll—"

"Save your breath," I said, "it—"

Which was when John Galey went and stuck his oar in.

"Figuring you suspected him of robbing the stage company was probably why Cuervo was making such a rumpus about you busting open Dall's safe, don't you reckon?"

"Too many turns in a Mex mind for me. As a matter of fact, an' just for the record, it was *me* caught *him* bustin' open Dall's safe; but too many of you fellas come tearin' in. I figured it wasn't no time for arguin'. You all figured I was the killer an' was slingin' your shots too close for comfort."

Tilt James' jaw was bogged wide open, but it didn't quite match what I read in his stare. And Curly Bill was swearing so mean it was almighty plain hell would get a chunk under it if he didn't quick learn who had blown Lou's light out.

"I'm arrestin' you, Whiskers," I said to Roach, "for killin' Lou Gromm, Hack Averill an' Cuervo. Got me fightin' my hat why you didn't get Tilt – but you're the guy all right. Just pass over that pistol you got stuck in your waistband."

There wasn't no sound; not a whisper of breath, even. Roach stared, amazed like.

Then a cold sneer lifted his lip and he

snorted.

John Galey said, "What in the world—?" and Milt Hicks snarled: "It's Tilt James you—"

"Oh, no it ain't." I said. "Gimme that gun, Roach."

Roach, with a leer, tossed his gun on the planking. Folding his arms he eyed me scornful.

"What'd you do with that shotgun?" I said.

"Never had no shotgun." Roach's yellow eyes jeered.

Curly Bill growled impatient: "You had this drifter locked up in your jail. He was still in his cell after Lou got killed. There ain't but two sets of keys. Don't talk like a nidjit! This guy never *knew* Lou—"

"That's where you're wrong," I grinned. "Harrigan's this guy's original handle – Dirk Harrigan. He's the famous 'brother' Weak Back was always runnin' off at the head about. Him an' Lou Gromm was real chummy once – pardners, in fact – till Lou run off with Dirk's woman one night. An' got Dirk grabbed by the Border Patrol. Caught him red-handed they did. Just like me—"

"You couldn't catch a cold!" Roach

171

sneered; and Curly Bill grunted uncharitably, "You got the same trouble's the rest of the starpackers – let a fella git into a jam some time an' you'll hound the pore fool fer the rest of his natcheral! You kin say what you like, but he never killed Lou – he *couldn't* of! You had him locked up in jail!"

I said, "Tilt – take a look at that gun he threw down. Hack Averill's, aint' it? . . . Thought so," I grinned. "Curl your ears, boys; I'm going t' tell you something. If Roach, like we figured, had stayed locked up in jail, it would be like you say; he couldn't of killed Lou. But he didn't stay locked up – *Lou let him out*. It's the only answer an' you can bet Lou done it.

" 'Cause why? Because I told Lou Gromm, that night 'fore I left, it was time we was lettin' Roach out, *muy pronto*. Since Roach got loose, Lou must of loosed him. Roach follored him back to the office. For his stuff. Lou give him his shotgun – must of gone to the desk for his other belongin's. Lou bent down to get 'em. Roach, never suspected on account of his whiskers, grabbed up my knife off—"

Roach was quick – but not quick enough.

He snatched the pistol from Milt Hicks' holster – came up with it roaring, the sound

172

of our shots crashing out simultaneous. But mine was first. Roach swayed and buckled.

"Don't worry," I told them. "I only creased him. He'll live to be swung when the Judge gets done with 'im.'"

When the rest was gone Tilt grabbed my hand. He worked it like he had hold of a pump. "By Gawd," he said, "you can move your truck out t' my place any time! 'F you come right now it won't be none too soon! There's a job f' you at the Cherrycows, Marlatt—"

"You can take your job an'—"

"Now, now . . ." Tilt said like I was just a button. "You done Tilt James a damn big favor, an' ol' Tilt ain't one—"

"You don't owe me a thing—"

"Don't *owe!*" Tilt roared. "You talk like a two-year-old! Craziest thing I ever done in my life was writin' that blasted note t' Dirk Harrigan! I musta been plumb outa my head! Lou locatin' all them gopherin' shop clerks – but I've got that minin' stuff all fixed up now. Bought John Galey plumb out, I have – lock, stock an' bar'l! I'm closin' the mine, an' the smelter, too – goin' t' close up this whole damn, stinkin' town! Just like I said I would! Just like I told that damn Lou Gromm!

"So there ain't goin' to be nothin' round here for you. You pack up yer things an' come out to the Cherrycows . . ."

I looked at Dora.

I said: "What the hell are we waitin' on, dammit!"

MAGNA-THORNDIKE hopes you have enjoyed this Large Print book. All our Large Print titles are designed for easy reading, and all our books are made to last. Other Magna Print or Thorndike Press books are available at your library, through selected bookstores, or directly from the publishers. For more information about current and upcoming titles, please call or mail your name and address to:

MAGNA PRINT BOOKS
Long Preston, Near Skipton,
North Yorkshire,
England BD23 4ND
(07294) 225

or in the USA

THORNDIKE PRESS
P.O. Box 159
Thorndike, Maine 04986
(800) 223-6121
(207) 948-2962
(in Maine and Canada call collect)

There is no obligation, of course.